Phillips Brooks, Frederic William Farrar

Daily Thoughts from Phillips Brooks

Phillips Brooks, Frederic William Farrar

Daily Thoughts from Phillips Brooks

ISBN/EAN: 9783337327248

Printed in Europe, USA, Canada, Australia, Japan

Cover: Foto ©Andreas Hilbeck / pixelio.de

More available books at **www.hansebooks.com**

FROM

PHILLIPS BROOKS

LATE BISHOP OF MASSACHUSETTS.

WITH ___ ESTIMATE AND _____ BY THE VENERABLE
____CHDEACO_ _____ D., F.R.S.

R. H. W_____ Y.

ESTIMATE AND TRIBUTE.

PHILLIPS BROOKS.

AN ESTIMATE AND TRIBUTE, BY THE VEN. ARCHDEACON
FARRAR, D.D., F.R.S.

IT was with a shock of grief that I read in the
American telegrams of January 23 the an-
nouncement of the death of my most dear and
honored friend, Phillips Brooks.   When I parted
from him at the end of last July it seemed immensely more likely that I—five years his senior
—should be called

"To where beyond these voices there is peace,"

than that he should pass away so suddenly from
the scene of his splendid activities.   He was a
man of magnificent physique—six feet five high
and strong and large in proportion.   His hand-
some features, his manly carriage, his striking
and massive head, his strong health, his vigorous

vii

personality, seemed to promise a long life to him
if to any man.   Every one, indeed, noticed during his last visit to England that he looked much
thinner than he had done two years before, but
he always spoke of himself as perfectly well, and
his great boyish heart seemed as full as ever of
love and hope and joy. · I noticed in him a just
perceptible deepening of gravity in tone, but no
diminution of his usually · bright spirits   He
resembled our common friend, the late Dean
Stanley, in the fact that his genius had all the
characteristics of " the heart of childhood taken
up and matured in the powers of manhood."   I
attributed the slightly less buoyant temperament
of last summer—the sort of half-sadness which
sometimes seemed to flit over his mind, like the
shadow of a summer cloud—to the exigencies
and responsibilities of his recent dignity.

For his work as a Bishop was to the last degree
exhausting.   He used to send me the printed list
of his engagements.   They were daily and in-

cessant. I stood amazed at them. They were, no doubt, greatly increased by his unprecedented popularity with the laity ; but to discharge them as he would discharge them must have required, and must, I fear, have impaired, a giant's strength. And this tax upon his powers, joined to the stress of a winter which has been terribly severe in America, must have hastened the end, which is for him so happy a release, but which to us seems so untimely a deprivation.

I cannot but think that if he had not accepted the call to the Bishopric of Massachusetts he might have lived for many a long and happy year. Assuredly it was not ambition which led him to desire such empty shadows as precedence and a title. I knew him too well to suppose that he would care a broken straw for such gilt fragments of potsherd, such dust in the midnight, as the worldly adjuncts of an inch-high distinction. His heart was too large for so small an ambition. Had he chosen to answer the world according to

its idols, to trim his sails to the veering breezes
of ecclesiastical opinion, to suppress or tamper
with his cherished convictions, and, as Tennyson
says, "to creep and crawl in the hedge-bottoms,"
he, with his rich gifts, might easily have been a
Bishop thirty years ago. In ability and every
commanding quality he towered head and shoulders above the whole body of American ecclesiastics, only one or two of whom are known outside their own parishes or dioceses. Probably no
severer lot could have befallen him than to be
made Bishop. For he was a man who had lived
a very happy life, and although he was in no
sense of the word indolent, he managed to escape
the entanglements of work which so disas-
trously crowd the lives of too many of us, not
only with harassing labors but also with endless
worry, fussy littlenesses and an infinite deal of
nothing. Wisely and rightly he left a margin to
his life, and did not crowd its pages to the very
edge. He enjoyed his quiet smoke and hour of

social geniality in the evening. He had an
insatiate love for travel. He had visited much
of what was best worth seeing in both hemis-
pheres, and wherever he went—being blessed
with admirable taste and ample means—he col-
lected memorials of his journeys. His bachelor
home in Boston—in which I twice spent happy
weeks—was full of careless beauty and solid comfort and was constantly brightened with the
presence of friends who loved him as few men
have been ever loved. His Episcopate must
have greatly altered the peaceful and joyous tenor
of his life. It must have exposed him to hun-
dreds of small vexations, which as they revealed
to him the inherent littleness of mankind—
especially as it displays itself in spheres ecclesiastical—must have put a severe strain on his faith
in human nature. I believe that he accepted his
so-called promotion solely for two reasons—
because he felt that to do so was a solemn duty
laid upon him, and because he hoped by this

self-sacrifice—not only of wealth and ease, but of things which he valued far more than both—to render real, high and most needful services to the church to which he belonged. I do not know that he was right. No man could do the work he has done and was doing, but much smaller men could have discharged the more ordinary functions of his new routine.

The following letter will show some of his feelings on his new appointment:

233 CLARENDON STREET, BOSTON, ⎱
May 19, 1891.   ⎰

DEAR DR. FARRAR: A thousand thanks for your most kind letter. I knew that I should have your sympathy!

I am not Bishop yet. We have a complicated constitution, and all the Dioceses and all the Bishops have to vote upon me before I am confirmed and can be consecrated. And so it will be some time yet; but it will come. Massachusetts has done its part, rather unexpectedly to everybody, and I shall probably be consecrated somewhere about October 1. It looks quite interesting and attractive, and I hope I shall not be quite useless in the new work which will occupy the remainder of my days. I have had a delightful life, and the last twenty years of it which I have spent in Trinity Church have been unbroken in their happiness. Why should I believe that the good Father has left me now, and has not made ready something good for me to do and be in these new fields? So I go on with good heart.

It will spoil any chance of my coming this year to Europe, and so I must not hope to preach in St. Margaret's. A quiet summer here at home, looking over the work, closing up the past and making ready for the future, is what evidently is appointed me. I am sorry for that. I do not like to let the years go by with so rare sights of friends' faces. And it will be long since I saw yours—another year, perhaps.

You know how constantly I think of you, and with what wonder and admiration I hear of your abounding labors, and with what deep sorrow I know of suffering that comes to you! It is a joy to me that you should put my name in your new book. It touches me and pleases me exceedingly.

And so, dear friend, may God's best blessing be to you and yours. My truest love to them.

And let me be always,

Affectionately your friend,

PHILLIPS BROOKS.

Whether, in addition to other trials, he suffered much from the malevolence of his opponents — whether he was in the slightest degree moved by reading such articles as that which was quoted in the last number of this REVIEW, in which the *Church Times*, with its usual exquisite amenity and that beautiful exhibition of the elementary Christian graces by which (in addition to infalli-bility) it is characterized—I do not know.   I think and hope that he was indifferent to what Montalembert calls "the unknown voices that bellow in the shade, and swell the language of falsehood and of hate."   What I do know is that in the cause of duty he feared, as little as I do myself, to encounter the daggers of masked "réligious" calumniators.   If he had to pass through veritable hurricanes of abuse from anony-mous critics, he could always turn from the storm without to the sunshine of "pure conscience within;" and he knew that he was enshrined in the enthusiastic affection of tens of thousands of

the brother Christians whom he had so nobly
served.

I never knew a man so supremely unaffected
by the

"Status, entourage, worldly circumstance"

of his episcopal rank.   It was with difficulty that
I persuaded him to wear in England his episcopal
robes, though any ordinary surplice looked ridi-
culous on his massive frame.   Once when I gave
the title, "my Lord," to dear old Bishop Lee, of
Delaware—then, I think, the Presiding American
Bishop—with whom I was staying, he quietly
said, "You are giving me, sir, a title to which I
have no claim."   What Phillips Brooks would
have done to me had I so addressed him I can
hardly conjecture.   I knew him too well to
make the attempt.   I have experienced in the
case of more than one man that when he becomes
a Bishop under the modern circumstances and
surroundings of that position, if he does not quite

" Bestride the narrow world
Like a Colossus,"

yet all the old familiar friendship is utterly at an
end. But his elevation did not make one atom
of difference in the case of Phillips Brooks. To
the last he was the dear, frank, manly, noble
Phillips Brooks, as humble, as cordial as ever.
He was too truly great to be merged in small
superiorities. All artificiality and all pretence
and all looking down upon others were to him impossible. Marcus Aurelius had to say to himself,
" Do not be Cæsarized." But Phillips Brooks
had no need of the warning not to be puffed up.
He was immensely greater than his bishopric. He
was too much of a man to be lost in the ecclesiastic. He did not develop that excess of caution
which leads some men to measure their words as
though they were the answers of an oracle, and
makes others so self-conscious and timid that they

" Dare not with too confident a tone
Proclaim the nose upon their face their own."

Such greatness as Phillips Brooks had lay in his true, large-hearted manhood ; and his manhood was too supreme to be artificialized into pomposity and euphuisms.

The letter which he wrote to me on December 13, his fifty-seventh and last birthday, lies before me. I print it here, omitting only a few words which his great kindness spoke. How strangely the words read to me, "I pray you to live !" The greater and the better is taken ; the feebler and less worthy is left.

233 CLARENDON STREET, BOSTON, }
Tuesday, December 13, 1892. }

MY DEAR ARCHDEACON: It is partly that I want to send you Christmas greeting, and partly that I need your sympathy to-day when I am fifty-seven years old—for these two reasons and a hundred others I am going to fill these four pages with talk with you across the water.

In the midst of a thousand useless things which I do every day there is always coming up the recollection of last summer, and how good you were to me, and what en-

2

joyment I had in those delightful idle days. Never shall
I cease to thank you for taking me to Tennyson's, and
letting me see the great dear man again. How good he
was that day! Do you remember how he read those two
stanzas about " Faith," which he had just written? I
can hear his great voice booming in them as I read them
over in the new volume which has come since the poet
died. And how perfect his death was! And how one
feels that he has brooded so on death, and grown familiar
with its mystery on every side, that it cannot have come
with surprise to him! And Whittier, too, is gone. He
never forgot the visit which you paid him, nor ceased to
speak of it whenever I saw him. But how strange it
seems, this writing against one friend's name after another
that you will see his face no more! I pray you to live, for
to come to London and not see you there, what should I
care for the old places, St. Margaret's, and the Abbey, and
the Dean's Yard, and all the rest?

I hope you know how I valued the sermons which I
heard from you in the Abbey on those Sunday afternoons
last summer. They have been in my ears and in my heart
ever since. Indeed, when I look back over these years, I
owe you very much indeed.

I hope that you are very well and happy. Do not let

the great world trouble you, but be sure that many are
rejoicing in your brave work.

O, that you were here to-night! With all best Christmas wishes for Mrs. Farrar and you and your children,

I am, affectionately your friend,

PHILLIPS BROOKS.

I first made his acquaintance about 16 years
ago. He called on me in Dean's Yard with his
brother. He brought no introduction, but
kindly came of his own accord to make my acquaintance. I asked Dean Stanley to appoint
him to preach in the Abbey, and he preached
on that occasion the sermon on "The Candle of
the Lord" which attracted such wide attention.
He had not then published any volume of sermons. I urged him to do so, and he complied,
naming the volume from the sermon by which
we had all been struck. That was the beginning
of many years of close friendship. His first visit
when he came to England was generally to my

house, and his first sermons were at St. Margaret's and the Abbey.

We in England were, of course, less familiar with his voice, and less able to catch his immensely rapid intonations than our American brethren. It was not only the rush of words which rendered it difficult to follow him, but the rush of thoughts. The two together made him the despair of reporters. Dean Stanley used to compare him to an express train going to its appointed terminus with majestic speed, and sweeping every obstacle, one after another, out of his course. I once tried to induce him to adopt a more measured utterance. He told me that for him it was absolutely impossible. In youth he had suffered from something resembling an impediment in his speech, and he could only preach rapidly, or not at all. He was supremely devoid of all self-consciousness in the pulpit. When an American clergyman was deploring to him the emptiness of many American churches,

he said, with the utmost simplicity, that it must
be quite a mistake, for wherever he preached he
founded all the churches quite full. It does not
seem to have occurred to him that it was his
name and fame and singular influence which attracted such large multitudes wherever he was
announced to preach.

He has given us his views on preaching in his
published lectures on the subject. The value of
his own sermons lay in their genuine manliness,
their sincerity of conviction, their freshness and
originality, their unity and directness of thought
their classic diction, and their brilliant illustrations. They contain sentences which, when we
have once read them, we never forget.

He generally preferred to read his sermons,
but he could preach equally well *extempore*, and
that without a note. Indeed, if the hearer shut
his eyes, he would have been unable to say
whether Phillips Brooks—as all Americans loved
to call him to the last—was preaching a written

or an unwritten sermon; he preached his old
sermons with as little reluctance as Dr. Chalmers.
I noticed on his MSS. that, even in his own
church, he often repeated the same sermon within
four years of its delivery. So far from resenting
this, his vast congregation liked it, and asked him
to preach again and again the same sermon. " I
am so glad that he preached *that* sermon at St.
Margaret's," said an American lady to me. " It
is a special favorite of ours at Boston."

In the present phase of ecclesiastical opinion,
what is called " Catholicity " is apparently regarded as identical with intolerance. It takes
its tones from the Papacy, and feebly echoes its
anti-Christian haughtiness and empty anathemas.
He in these days is supposed to be the best
"Catholic" and the most faithful "Churchman"
who turns his back most contumeliously on his
Christian brethren who are not of the same fold
as himself, and shows the greatest amount of
hesitation even in handing them over to the

possibility of "uncovenanted mercies." The Christianity of Phillips Brooks was not of this narrow, repellent, sacerdotal, and Popish type. He deliberately and constantly committed the crime, so unpardonable in the eyes of the new tyranny, of regarding all his fellow-Christians, to whatever denomination they belonged, as no less honest, and no less dear to God than himself— as the heirs with him of the common mysteries of redemption and immortality, the children with him of a common Father, the redeemed with him of a common Saviour, the sheep with him of one flock, though in different folds, fellow-heirs with him of a common and unexclusive heaven. Like Henri Peyrrève, he hated to see churches make their gates bristle with razors and anathemas. He would have said with St. Irenæus, *Ubi Christus ibi Ecclesia.* He did not explain away the plain words of Christ: "Where two or three are gathered together in My name, there am I in the midst of them."

He had not ceased to attach any meaning to the words, "When Thou hadst overcome the sharpness of death, Thou didst open the kingdom of Heaven to all believers." He would have said with the Abbess Angélique Arnauld, "I am of the Church of all the saints, and all the saints are of my Church." Where he saw the fruits of the Spirit he was convinced of the presence of the Spirit, and no loud assertion made him believe that that Spirit was present in factions which yield only the fruits of bitterness, and are chiefly conspicuous for the broad phylacteries of uncharitable arrogance.

Religious animosity might bark at his heels, but he was so inherently noble in himself that it did not make him lose his faith, his hope, his love, his courage, nor did it ever cause him to swerve a hair's breadth from the inflexible line on which he saw that his duty lay. And he had his reward. His opponents will subside into their native insignificance and be forgotten, ex-

cept so far as the accident of connecting themselves with his name will preserve them from
oblivion. His name will live for many a long
year as the name of the foremost of all American
ecclesiastics of this generation; as the name of a
man whose manhood and whose sweet and lofty
character won, and as Americans would say,
" magnetized " to an unprecedented extent, all
true hearts. Outside of sacerdotal cliques, every
one knew, every one admired, every one loved
Phillips Brooks. He was the common property,
the common enthusiasm of the great American
nation. The great writers of America recognized him, and him only among clerics, as their
intellectual peer. At his house, and at the
Saturday Club, I have dined with Mr. Lowell
and Dr. O. W. Holmes, and many of the Americans who were foremost in literary, scientific and
political circles, and he was always the favorite of
all. The venerable Quaker poet, J. G. Whittier,
treated him like a brother. In all this his life

was very enviable, but perhaps most of all in the influence which he wielded over the hearts of young men. I was with him at Harvard, at Yale, at Portland, at Syracuse, and at other American schools and universities. As the guest and stranger, it always fell to me to address those eager young students; but when I had finished, if Phillips Brooks was with me on the platform, "the boys" always shouted for him, and would not leave off till he had said a few words to them. Often what he said was perfectly simple, and was in no way striking. I do not remomber the topic of his little speeches any more than I remember my own, but when he had spoken to them "the boys" were always satisfied, for they always felt that they had been listening to a man.

Nothing was more remarkable in him than his royal optimism. With him it was a matter of faith and temperament. He had not had to fight his way into it as, perhaps, Browning had—whom among other great Englishmen I had the pleasure of introducing to him. I think he must have been born an optimist. But often, when I was inclined to despond, his conversation, his bright spirits, his friendliness, his illimitable hopes came to me like a breath of vernal air. He rejoiced to have been born in this century because of its large outlook ; and when he became godfather to one of my grandchildren, he wrote that the children were to be envied whose lot would be cast in an epoch which he believed would be rendered glorious by discoveries and progress even more memorable than those which have marked our own.

He is gone. He has left the world much poorer for his loss. All that is best, every element that is not ignoble in the American church, has special cause to grieve his irreparable loss. There is not one ecclesiastic in America whose death could cause anything like so deep a sorrow, or create anything like so immense a void. Would to God that we had a few men such as he

in the English church. I have known many
men—even not a few clergymen—of higher
genius, of far wider learning, of far more brilliant gifts. But I never met any man, or any
ecclesiastic, half so natural, so manly, so large-
hearted, so intensely Catholic in the only real
sense, so loyally true in his friendships, so absolutely unselfish, so modest, so unartificial, so self-
forgetful. He is gone, and I for one never hope
to look upon his like again. To have known
him, to have been honored by his friendship, to
have witnessed his noble life and his large aspira-
tions, consoles me much. It is in itself "a
liberal education." And now that his lot is
among the saints, who would wish him back
amid all the pettiness and baseness and strife of
tongues, which are, alas! quite as common in
the nominal Church as in the authentic world?
A blessing and a gracious presence has vanished
out of many lives. With a very sad heart I bid
him farewell and lay this "shadow of a wreath of

lilies '' on the fresh grave of the noblest, truest
and most stainless man I ever knew.*

* By the kind permission of the editors of the " Review
of Reviews " we are enabled to give this estimate and tribute of Bishop Brooks.

DAILY THOUGHTS.

January 1.

Will you let Christ tell you what is the perfect man? Will you let Him set His simplicity and graciousness close to your life, and will you feel their power? Oh! be brave, be true, be pure, be men, be men in the power of Jesus Christ. May God bless you! May God bless you!

January 2.

Men have found what Jesus was perpetually declaring, what Jesus was more and more declaring as He came into the fuller consciousness of His own life, that in Him and His experience, in His soul, there lay the solution of every problem, the enlightenment of every darkness—the darknesses which should yet arise, the darknesses which are to come as men move into fuller light. For it is the law of progress that as men move into the light they realize more fully the measure of darkness which lies about them, and feel the need of still richer truths to lead them into the light which lies beyond.

January 3.

Shall there be no Christ for the strong men who have before them the duties of their life, and who want the strength with which to do them? Shall there be no Christ for the young men, the young men standing in danger, but also standing in such magnificent and splendid chances? It is great to think of Christ standing by the sorrowing and comforting them. It is great,—we will not say it is greater,—it is very great, when by the side of the young man just entering into life there stands the Christ, saying to his soul, with the voice that he cannot fail to hear: " Be pure, be strong, be wise, be independent; rejoice in Me and My appreciation. Let the world go, if it is necessary that the world should go. Serve the world, but do not be the servant of the world. Make the world your servant by helping the world in every way in which you can minister to its life. Be brave, be strong, be manly by My strength.''

January 4.

The purpose and result of freedom is service. It sounds to us at first like a contradiction, like a paradox. Great truths very often present themselves to us in the first place as paradoxes, and it is only when we come to combine the two different terms of which they are composed and see how it is only by their meeting that the truth does reveal itself to us, that the truth does become known. It is by this same truth that God frees our souls, not from service, not from duty, but into service and into duty, and he who makes mistakes the purpose of his freedom mistakes the character of his freedom.

January 5.

The highest conception of the state, as of the world, is that it is an uttered thought of God, a certain colossal utterance of truth.

January 6.

Duty has become to us such a hard word, service has become to us a word so full of the spirit of bondage, that it surprises us at the first moment when we are called upon to realize that it is in itself a word of freedom. And yet we constantly are lowering the whole thought of our being, we are bringing down the greatness and richness of that with which we have to deal, until we recognize that God does not call us to our fullest life simply for ourselves.

We know it at once if we turn to Him who represents the fulness of the nature of our humanity.

January 7.

Let your eye be upon the light which, through

every jungle, will beat its way to the soul that is looking for it, and show that soul that it essentially belongs to God.

January 8.

The great question that is on men's minds to-day, as I believe it has never been upon men's minds before, is this: Is this Christian religion, with its high pretensions, this Christian life that claims so much for itself, is it competent for the task that it has undertaken to do? Can it meet all these human problems, and relieve all these human miseries, and fulfil all these human hopes?

Christian men, it is for us to give our bit of answer to that question. It is for us, in whom the Christian Church is at this moment partially embodied, to declare that Christianity, that the Christian faith, the Christian manhood, can do that for the world which the world needs. You say, "What can I do?" You can furnish one Christian life. You can furnish a life so faithful to every duty, so ready for every service, so

determined not to commit every sin, that the
great Christian Church shall be the stronger for
your living in it, and the problem of the world
be answered.

January 9.

Oh, this marvellous, this awful power that we
have over other people's lives! Oh! the power
of the sin that you have done years and years
ago! It is awful to think of it. I think there
is hardly anything more terrible to the human
thought than this—the picture of a man who,
having sinned years and years ago in a way that
involved other souls in his sin, and then, having
repented of his sin and undertaken another life,
knows certainly that the power, the consequence
of that sin is going on outside of his reach, beyond even his ken and knowledge. No steps,
quickened with all your earnestness, can pursue
it. No contrition can draw back its consequences.
Remorse cannot force the bullet back again into
gun from which it once has gone forth. It makes

life awful to the man who has ever sinned, who has ever wronged and hurt another life because of this sin, because no sin ever was done that did not hurt another life.

January 10.

Thank God that when a man does a bit of service, however little it may be, of that too he can never trace the consequences. Thank God for that which in some better moment, in some nobler inspiration, you did ten years ago to make your brother's faith a little more strong. To establish the purity of a soul instead of staining it and shaking it, thank God, in this quick, electric atmosphere in which we live, that, too, runs forth. Do not say in your terror, "I will do nothing." You must do something. Only let Christ tell you—let Christ tell you that there is nothing that a man rests upon in the moment, that he thinks of, as he looks back upon it when it has sunk into the past, with any satisfaction, except some service to his fellow-men, some strengthening and helping of a human soul.

January 11.

That is the Christian life, the following of Jesus Christ.

January 12.

God wastes no history. In every age and every land He is working for the elucidation of some moral truth, some riper culture for the character of man.

January 13.

Christianity has not yet been tried. My friends, no man dares to condemn the Christian faith to-day, because the Christian faith has not been tried. Not until men get rid of the thought that it is a poor machine, an expedient for saving them from suffering and pain, not until they get the grand idea of it as the great power of God present in and through the lives of men, not until then does Christianity enter upon its true trial and become ready to show what it can do. Therefore, we may struggle against our sin in order that men may be saved around us, and not simply that our own souls may be saved.

January 14.

It is impossible, as I have suggested to you again and again in what I have been saying, that a man can have his mind open to the receipt of the truth of a person unless he be a certain kind of man himself. I do not know but the basest and wickedest man who lives may believe in the Copernican theory, or that two and two make four, yet I cannot help believing that if he were a better and truer man he would believe even those truths, outside of himself, of science and arithmetic, more fully and deeply. Men were not all astray in the first thing that they were seeking after, though they were wofully astray in many things that they said about it, when they talked about faith and works. Faith enters in through the soul that does a noble deed, and in the coming in of that faith the higher deed be-comes possible to him.

January 15.

When I turn to Jesus and think of Him as the manifestation of His own Christianity—and if men would only look at the life of Jesus to see what Christianity is, and not at the life of the poor representatives of Jesus whom they see around them, there would be so much more clearness, they would be rid of so many difficul-ties and doubts. When I look at the life of Jesus I see that the purpose of consecration, of emancipation, is service of His fellow-men.

January 16.

•

There is a certain widespread nervousness and fear of giving force any true place in the world. It seems a horrible intruder, soon, we pray, to be cast out. And yet force is as truly the companion of reason as body is of spirit. Righteous force is the reaction of truth upon opposing matter.

January 17.

I cannot think for a moment of Jesus as doing that which so many religious people think they are doing when they serve Christ, when they give their lives to Him. I cannot think of Him as simply saving His own soul, living His own life, and completing His own nature in the sight of God. It is a life of service from beginning to end. He gives himself to man because He is absolutely the child of God, and He sets up service, and nothing but service, to be the ultimate purpose, the one great desire, on which the souls of His followers should be set, as His own soul is set, upon it continually.

January 18.

That men should be true to their best convictions, and to their simple duty, this is the blessing that gives all blessings with it, and is the fountain of all charity and progress.

January 19.

He who thinks that he is being released from the work, and not set free in order that he may accomplish that work, mistakes the Christ from whom the freedom comes, mistakes the condition into which his soul is invited to enter.

For if the freedom of a man simply consists in the larger opportunity to be and to do all that God makes him in His creation capable of being and doing, then certainly if man has been capable of service it is only by the entrance into service, by the acceptance of that life of service for which God has given man the capacity, that he enters into the fulness of his freedom and becomes the liberated child of God.

January 20.

Truths are the roots of duties. A rootless

duty, one that has no truth below it out of which it grows, has no life, and will have no growth.

January 21.

The thing that impresses me more and more is this—that we only need to have extended to the multitude that which is at this moment present in the few, and the world really would be saved. There is but the need of the extension into a multitude of souls of that which a few souls have already attained in their consecration of themselves to human good, and to the service of God, and I will not say the millennium would have come, but heaven would have come, the new Jerusalem would be here.

January 22.

The Church has been spread by force, but Christianity never. To try to think of extending a faith by force is to try to think a contradiction. It is like thinking of raising enthusiasm with levers, or crushing genius with sledge hammers. The tools have no relation to the material or the task.

January 23.

Any man or any institution which attempts a great religious work in behalf of the growing generations of a country, must undertake as preparatory to it, and as a necessary part of it, a great moral work as well. A faithful ministry, we hold, must not merely declare the Saviour, but must attack and beat down those special sins which stand in the very doorways and keep the Saviour out of the hearts of men.

January 24.

It is the joy of service that makes the life of Christ, and for us to serve Him, serving fellow-man and God—as He served fellow-man and God—whether it bring pain or joy, if we can only get out of our souls the thought that it matters not if we are happy or sorrowful, if only we are dutiful and faithful, and brave and strong, then we should be in the atmosphere, we should be in the great company of the Christ.

January 25.

It is not your business and mine to study whether we shall get to heaven, even to study whether we shall be good men; it is our business to study how we shall come into the midst of the purposes of God and have the unspeakable privilege in these few years of doing something of His work. And yet so is our life all one, so is the kingdom of God which surrounds us and infolds us one bright and blessed unity, that when a man has devoted himself to the service of God and his fellow-man, immediately he is thrown back upon his own nature, and he sees now—it is the right place for him to see—that he must be the brave, strong, faithful man, because it is impossible for him to do his duty and to render his service, except it is rendered out of a heart that is full of faithfulness, that is brave and true.

January 26.

Thought is not simply the sea upon which the world of action rests, but, like the air which pervades the whole solid substance of our globe, it permeates and fills it in every part. It is thought which gives to it its life. It is thought which makes the manifestation of itself in every different action of man. I hope we are not so deluded as men have been sometimes, as some men are to-day, that we shall try to separate these two lives from one another, and one man say, " Everything depends upon my action, and I care not what I think," or, as men have said, at least, in other times, "If I think right, it matters not how I act." But the right thought and the right action make one complete and single man.

January 27.

Only when Christianity is a force, only when I seek independence of men in serving men, do I cease to be a slave to their whims.

January 28.

We make very much of free thought in these days. Let us always remember that free thought means the opportunity to think, and not the opportunity not to think. We rejoice in the way in which our fathers came to this country and in their children perpetuated the purpose of their coming, in order that they might have freedom to worship God. Do we worship God? Simply to have attained freedom and not to use freedom for its true purpose, not to live within the world of freedom according to the life which is given to us there—that is to do dishonor to the freedom, to disown the purpose for which the freedom has been given to us.

January 29.

Once accept the supreme importance of truth, and every part of our nature becomes anxious for the preservation of the testimonies of God. The

4

great doctrines of our faith become the great
pillars of our life.

January 30.

Perfect truth consists not merely in the right
constituents of character, but in their right and
intimate conjunction.   This union of the mental
and moral into a life of admirable simplicity is
what we most admire in children, but in them it
is unsettled and unpractical.   But when it is pre-
served into a manhood, deepened into reliability
and maturity, it is that glorified childlikeness,
that high and reverend simplicity which shames
and baffles the most accomplished astuteness, and
is chosen by God to fill his purposes when he
needs a ruler for his people of faithful and true
heart.

January 31.

Truth and nature are in their very nature
mighty and intolerant, and must fight with and
conquer falsehood and sin in any region of this
many-regioned universe where they may meet.

February 1.

Christianity is one and everlasting. Its work of salvation for man's soul is the same blessed work forever. But its relation to the world's life at large must be forever changing with the changes of that world's needs and seekings. The larger applications of Christianity must of necessity be from time to time readjusted, and in their readjustments its power may be temporarily obscured or unrecognized as it passes into new forms of exhibition.

February 2.

Through our fathers' wisdom and devotion, we must become wiser and more devoted than they. Friends, we must rise to thoughts beyond our fathers, or we are not our fathers' worthy children. Not to do in our days just what our fathers did long ago, but to live as truly up to our light as our fathers lived up to theirs,—that is what it is to be worthy of our fathers.

February 3.

Men talk about morality as one thing, and religion as another. Sometimes they pit them one against the other, as if they were some sort of natural antagonism between the two. There can be no such thing as morality without religion, and morality becomes more and more genuine just in proportion as religion becomes more and more sound and true. We do not believe in any reform which finds its whole motive within the region of human relations. We look for the permanent success of no effort, however noble its appointed aim may be, which does not draw its impulse from some association of humanity with a power and a will above its own.

February 4.

Life can only be truly communicated by truly living methods. Nothing else will do. This takes all power away from mere machineries, from the highest to the lowest.

February 5.

I know no man's nature finally but by that testimony which the nature gives me of him. Bring me all evidence that the man is trustworthy, and then when I am convinced I will go and stand in the presence of that man himself, and he shall tell me. So the world stood, so the world stands to-day in the presence of Jesus Christ. His presence on earth is an historic fact. The words that He spoke are written down in a true record. The deeds that He did are the history of the manifestations of His character, and the story of His christendom is the continued manifestation of His life, the divine life in the life of man, made divine through Him.

February 6.

Religion is not something that is fastened upon the outside of life, but is the awakening of the truth inside of life.

February 7.

But what, then, is the Christian religion? It is the simple following of the divine person, Jesus Christ, who, entering into our humanity, has made evident two things—the love of God for that humanity, and the power of that humanity to answer to the love of God. The one thing that the eye of the Christian sees and never can lose is that majestic, simple figure, great in its simplicity, in its innocence, in its purity and in its unworldliness, that walked once on this earth and that walks forever through the lives of men, showing Himself to human kind, manifest in human kind. The power to receive it, the divine life wakened in every child of man by the divine life manifested in Jesus Christ. That is the great Christian faith, and the man becomes a Christian in his belief when he assures himself that that manifestation of the divine life has been made and is perpetually being made, and he answers to that appeal of the Christ.

February 8.

This truth comes to us more and more the longer that we live, that on what field or in what uniform, or with what aims we do our duty, matters very little, or even what our duty is, great or small, splendid or obscure. Only to find our duty certainly and somewhere, somehow do it faithfully, makes us good, strong, happy, and useful men, and tunes our lives into some feeble echo of the life of God.

February 9.

Of the essential life of the Church, of the truly living Church, what can we say but this? That it is that which most completely feels that it was made for men, not men for it; which, therefore, lives only as it lives in them; which strives for nothing but to open more and more the channels of life from Christ to them?

February 10.

I say that only when a man puts himself where

he can feel the power of Christ, where it is possible for him, if there be a Christ, if Christ be all
that the Christian religion claims that He is,
only when a man puts himself where he needs
and must have and must certainly feel that Christ,
if there be a Christ, only then has he a right to
disbelieve if the Christ be not there, only then
has he a right to believe if the Christ find him
there.   And where is that?   When a man takes
up the highest duties, when   he accepts the
noblest life, when he lays open his soul to the
great exactions and obligations which belong to
him in his spiritual nature, when he tries to be a
pure man, a devoted man, a noble man, only
then has he a chance to know that force which
only then comes into its activity.

February 11.

Hear the words that Jesus said, words that
our age must take to itself until it shall be wiser
than it is to-day : " Blessed are the pure in heart,

for they shall see God." '" If any man will do His will, he shall know of the doctrine, whether it be of God." Ponder those words, my friends. See how reasonable they are. See how important they are. See how they have the secret of your own life, of what it is to do, of what it is to be, forever and ever sealed up in them. These two things, I am sure, are true with regard to the method of belief—that no man can ever go forward to a higher belief until he is true to the faith which he already holds. Be the noblest man that your present faith, poor and weak and imperfect as it is, can make you to be. Live up to your present growth, your present faith. So, and so only, as you take the next straight step forward, as you stand strong where you are now, so only can you think the curtain will draw back and there will be revealed to you what lies beyond.

February 12.

I do not know how any man can stand and plead

with his brethren for the higher life, that they
will enter into and make their own the life of
Christ and God, unless he is perpetually conscious that around them with whom he pleads
there is the perpetual pleading and the voice of
God himself.   *   *   *   *   But if it be so, that
God is pleading with every one of His children
to enter into the highest life ; if it be so, that
God is making His application and His appeal to
every soul to know Him, and in Him to know
himself, then one may plead with earnestness and
plead with great hopefulness before his brethren.
And so it is.   The great truth of Jesus Christ is
that, that God is pleading with every soul, not
merely in the words which we hear from one another, not merely in the words which we read
from His book, but in every influence of life ;
and, in those unknown influences which are
too subtle for us to understand or perceive,
God is forever seeking after the souls of His children.

February 13.

Believe that the highest you ever have been you may be all the time, and vastly higher still if only the power of the Christ can occupy you and fill your life all the time.

February 14.

Only when a man tries to live the divine life can the divine Christ manifest Himself to him. Therefore the true way for you to find Christ is not to go groping in a thousand books.   It is not for you to try evidences about a thousand things that people have believed of Him, but it is for you to undertake so great a life, so devoted a life, so pure a life, so serviceable a life, that you cannot do it exactly by Christ, and then see whether Christ helps you.   See whether there comes to you the certainty that you are a child of God, and the manifestation of the child of God becomes the most credible, the most certain thing to you in all of history.

February 15.

Man stands separated from that life of God, as it were, by a great, thick wall, and every effort to put away his sin, to make himself a nobler and a purer man, is simply his beating at the inside of that door which stands between him and the life of God, which he knows that he ought to be living. And the glory and the beauty of it is that while he is beating upon the inside of the wall there is also a noble power praying upon the outside of the wall. The life to which he ought to come is striving in its turn, upon its side, to break away the hindrance that is keeping him from the thing he ought to be, that is keeping him from the life he ought to live. God, with His sunshine and lightning, with the great majestic manifestations of Himself, and with all the peaceful exhibitions of His life, is forever trying, upon His side of the wall, to break away the great barrier that separates the sinner's life from Him.

February 16.

Can there be anything more winning to the soul, anything that brings a deeper shame to you, than to have it revealed to you, suddenly or slowly, that from the first day that you came into this world, nay, before your life was an uttered fact in this world, God has been loving you, and seeking you, and planning for you, and making every effort that He could make in consistency with the free will with which He endowed you from the centre of His own life, that you might become His and therefore might become truly yourself? Through all the years in which you were obstinate and rebellious, through all the years in which you defied Him, nay, through the years in which you denied Him and said that He did not exist, He was with you all the time.

February 17.

Life is the thing we seek, and man finds it in the fulfilment of his life by Jesus Christ.

February 18.

Shall it not be so to-day, and shall it not be the truth, upon which we let our minds especially dwell, and which we keep in our souls all the time, that however He may be hidden from our sight God is the ultimate fact and the final purpose and power of the universe, and that everything that man tries to do for his fellow-man is but the expression of that love of God which is everywhere struggling to utter itself in blessing, to give itself away to the soul of every one for whom He cares?

February 19.

It is one of the signs to me of how human words are constantly becoming perverted that it surprises us when we think of freedom as a condition in which a man is called upon to do, and is enabled to do, the duty that God has laid upon him.

February 20.

I honor the sceptic, the faithful and devout sceptic, with all my soul. I am no scorner of the man who, without scorn, finds it impossible to accept that which to my soul seems to be the absolute truth. I will scorn only that which God scorns. He scorns the scorner, and only the scorning man is worthy of the scorn of human kind. But while I honor the sceptic, while I invite him to make manifest his scepticism, not merely for his sake but for my own, I will not hold, I cannot hold that he is living a larger life than the man whom the Christ invites to every noble duty, to every faithful fulfilment of himself.

February 21.

God is everywhere giving himself to us, the opening of the windows is a signal that we want him and an invitation that He will be glad enough to answer, to come. Into every window that is open to Him and turned His way, Christ comes, God comes.

February 22.

There is no soul so black in its sinfulness, so determined in its defiant obstinacy, that God has abandoned his throne room at the centre of the sinner's life, and every movement is the God movement and every effort is the God force, with which man tries to break forth from his sin and come forth into the full sunlight of a life with God. Do you not think how full of hope it is ? Do you not see that when this great conception of the universe, which is Christ's conception, which beamed in every look that He shed upon the world, which was told in every word that He spoke and which was in every movement of His hand—do you not see how, when this great conception of the universe takes possession of a man, then all his struggle with his sin is changed. it becomes a strong struggle, a glorious struggle. He hears perpetually the voice of Christ, "Be of good cheer. I have overcome the world. You shall overcome it by the same strength which overcame with Me.".

February 23.

When man is bidden to look back into his humanity and see what it means to be a man, that humanity means purity, truthfulness, earnestness, and faithfulness to that God of which humanity is a part, that God which manifested that humanity was a part of it, when the incarnation showed how close the divine and human belonged together—when man hears that voice, I do not know how he can resist, why he shall not lift himself up and say, " Now I can be a man, and I can be man only as I share in and give my obedience to and enter into communion with the life of God," and say to Christ, to Christ the revealer of all this, "Here I am, fulfil my manhood."

February 24.

God gives Himself to every soul that wants Him and declares its want by the open readiness of the signal which He knows.

5

February 25.

What shall be our universal law of life? Can we give it as we draw toward our last moment? I think we can. I want to live, I want to live, if God will give me help, such a life that, if all men in the world were living it, this world would be regenerated and saved. I want to live such a life that, if that life changed into new personal peculiarities as it went to different men, but the same life still, if every man were living it, the millenium would be here; nay, heaven would be here, the universal presence of God. Are you living that life now? Do you want your life multiplied by the thousand million so that all men shall be like you, or don't you shudder at the thought, don't you give hope that other men are better than you are? Keep that fear, but only that it may be the food of a diviner hope, that all the world may see in you the thing that man was meant to be, that is, the Christ.

February 26.

It is interesting to see how all that is true in regard to the matter of belief, doctrine, and opinions which we are apt to accept. How strange it very often seems that men go to the Church, or to one another, and say: "Must I believe this doctrine in order that I can enter into the Church?" "Must I believe this doctrine in order that I may be saved?" men say with a strange sort of notion about what salvation is. How strange it seems, when we really have got our intelligence about us and know what it is to believe! To believe a new truth, if it be really truth and we really believe it, is to have entered into a new region, in which our life shall find a new expansion and a new youth. Therefore, not "Must we believe?" but "May I believe?" is the true cry of the human creature who is seeking for the richest fulfilment of his life, who is working that his whole nature may find its complete expansion and so its completest exercise.

February 27.

To make life as successful as you can, you should not go away by yourself and say that you will live a good life, and then do nothing else. To cherish self is not the way to do service. You must lose self. Make yourself so strongly a part of the whole world that you influence all the other parts, and the more strongly cement them together. Take in some other life. Serve it and show it that there is a divine image hidden in it. Develop that image, and in so doing you beautify your own life.

February 28.

Nothing is completely good that is not infinite.

February 29.

Be your own best self, for the good of your fellow-men.

March 1.

It seems to me, my friends, that all this great

picture of the liberty into which Christ sets man, in the first place does one thing which we are longing to see done in the world. It takes away the glamor and the splendor from sin. It breaks that spell by which men think that the evil thing is the glorious thing. If the evil thing be that which Christ has told us that the evil thing is— which I have no time to tell you now—if every sin that you do is not simply a stain upon your soul, but is keeping you out from some great and splendid thing which you might do, then is there any sort of splendor and glory about sin?

March 2.

Never dare to touch any man's life without the most perfect and absolute reverence, because you are touching the most sacred thing that is in this world.

March 3.

Oh! how this world has perverted words and meanings, that the mastery of Jesus Christ should

seem to be the imprisonment and not the enfran-
chisement of the soul!   When I bring a flower
out of the darkness and set it in the sun, and let
the sunlight come streaming down upon it, and
the flower knows the sunlight for which it was
made and opens its fragance and beauty; when I
take a dark pebble and put it into the stream and
let the silver water go coursing down over it and
bringing forth the hidden color that was in the
bit of stone, opening the nature that is in them,
the flower and stone rejoice.   I can almost hear
hear them sing in the field and in the stream.
What then?   Shall not man bring his nature out
into the fullest illumination, and surprise himself
by the things that he might do?   Oh! the littleness of the lives that we are living! Oh! the way
in which we fail to comprehend, or when we do
comprehend, deny to ourselves the bigness of that
thing which it is to be a man, to be a child of God!

March 4.

What is the Christian?   Everywhere the man

who, so far as he comprehends Jesus Christ, so far as he can get any knowledge of Him, is His servant, the man who makes Christ the teacher of his intelligence and the guide of his soul, the man who obeys Christ as far as he has been able to understand Him. What, you say, the man who imperfectly understands Christ, who don't know anything about His divinity, who denies the great doctrines of the Church in regard to Him, is he a Christian? Certainly he is, my friends. There is no other test than this, the following of Jesus Christ.

March 5.

Let yourselves never think that you grow liberal in faith by believing less; always be sure that the true liberality of faith can only come by believing more.

March 6.

There is no single act of your life, my friend, there is no single dilemma in which you find yourself placed, in which the answer is not in Jesus Christ.

March 7.

Ask yourself of any habit that belongs to your own personal life, and bring it face to face with Jesus Christ and see if it is not judged. A judgment day that is far away, that is off in the dim distance when this world is done—it shall come, no doubt. I know none of us can know much with regard to it, except that it is sure. . But the judgment day that is here now is Christ; the judgment day that is right close to your life and rebukes you, if you will let Him rebuke you every time you sin, the judgment day that is here and praises you and bids you be of good courage, when you do a thing that men disown and despise, is Christ.

March 8.

Have you ever thought of how the world has stood in glory and honor before the sinless humanity of Jesus Christ? If any life could prove, if any argument could show on investigation to-day that Jesus did one sin in all his life, that the perfect liberty which was His perfect purity was not absolutely perfect, do you realize what a horror would seem to fall down from the heavens, what a constraint and burden would be laid upon the lives of men, how the gates of men's possibilities would seem to close in upon them? It is because there has been that one life which, because absolutely pure from sin, was absolutely free; it is because man may look up and see in that life the revelation and possibility of his own; it is because that life echoing the great cry throughout the world that man everywhere is the son of God, offers the same purity—and so the same freedom —to all mankind; it is for that reason that a man rejoices to cling to, to believe in, however impure his life is, the perfect purity, the sinlessness of the life of Jesus.

March 9.

The Christian faith is not a dogma, it is not primarily a law, but is a personal presence and an immediate llfe that is right here and now.

March 10.

Jesus Christ, the comforter of sorrow. He is the comforter of sorrow, for he knew and he knows what sorrow is. In his own crucifixion, in that which came before His crucifixion, He knew the suffering of this earthly life. There is no human being who ever has known the misery of man as Jesus knows it, and so He comes to all sorrows with tender consolation. God grant, God grant He may come to any of you who have come into these doors to-day with a sorrow, with a fear, with a dread upon your hearts, with souls that are wrung, with bodies that are suffering! God grant that the Christ may comfort you, may comfort you.

March 11.

The old legend was that the clothes of the Israelites which the Bible said waxed not old upon them in the desert during those forty years, not merely waxed not old those forty years, but grew with their growth, so that the little Hebrew who crossed the Red Sea in his boy's clothes wore the same clothes when he entered into the Promised Land. It is the parable of that which comes to the man who has a true Christian faith, a faith which comes in the personal friendship of Christ, a faith which comes not in the belief of certain things about Him, not in the doing slavishly of certain things which it seemed as if it had been said by Him that we must do, but in the personal entrance into His nature in a life for Him, in which he is able to send His life down into us.

March 12.

How that idea has haunted men in every period of their existence, how it is haunting you, that there is some higher life which it is possible to live! There has never been a religion that has not started there, lifted up its eyes and seen, afar off, what it was possible for man to do from day to day, in contrast with the things which men

immediately and presently are.   There is not any
moment of the human soul which has not rested
upon some great conception that man has a
nobler being than he was ordinarily conceiving
himself to be ; that he was not destined to the
things which were ordinarily occupying his life ;
that he might be living a greater and nobler life.
It is because the Christian Scriptures have laid
most earnestly hold of this idea, it is because it
was represented not simply in the words which
Christ said, but in the very being which Christ
was, that we go to them to get the inspiration
and the indication, the revelation and the enlightenment which we need.

March 13.

As the man walks up the mountain, he seems
to pass out of the cloud which hangs about the
lower slopes of the mountain, until at last he
stands upon the pinnacle at the top, and there is
in the perfect light.   Is it not exactly like the

mountain at whose foot there seems to be the open sunshine where men see everything, and on whose summit there is the sunshine, but on whose sides, and half way up, there seems to linger a long cloud, in which man has to struggle until he comes to the full result of his life? So it is with self-consecration, with service. You easily do it in some small ways in the lower life. Life becomes intensified and earnest with a serious purpose, and it seems as if it gathered itself together into selfishness. Only then it opens by and by into the largest and noblest works of men, in which they most manifest the richness of their human nature and appropriate the strength of God.

March 14.

Pray. Yes go to the God whom you but dimly see and pray to Him in the darkness, where He seems to sit. Ask Him, as if He were, that He will give you that which, if He is, must come from Him, can come from him alone. Pray anxiously. Pray passionately, in the simplest of all words, with the simplest of all thoughts. Pray, the manliest thing that a man can do, the fastening of his life to the eternal, the drinking of his thirsty soul out of the great fountain of life. And pray distinctly. Pray upon your knees. One grows tired sometimes of the free thought, which is yet perfectly true, that a man can pray anywhere and anyhow. But men have found it good to make the whole system pray. Kneel down, and the very bending of these obstinate and unused knees of yours will make the soul kneel down in the humility in which it can be exalted in the sight of God.

March 15.

Christ is the very embodiment of human liberty. In His own personal life and in everything that He did and said, He was forever uttering the great gospel that man, in order to become his completest, must become his freest, that what a man did when he entered into a new life was to open a new region in which new powers were to find their exercise, in which he was to be able to be and do things which he could not be and do in more restricted life. It is the acceptance of that idea, it seems to me, that makes us true disciples of Christ and of that great gospel, and that transfigures everything.

March 16.

"As many as received Him, to them gave He power to become the sons of God."

Just think of it!—the sons of God! The power to become that to as many as will receive the present Christ.

March 17.

Do not let yourselves say, that the man who gives himself to Jesus Christ and earnestly tries to enter in deeper and deeper into his life and tries to do his will, that he may know the Christ and know himself in the Christ more and more—dare not call that brother a fool, as you have some-

times called your Christian man who watched
scrupulously over his life and prayed. When a
man for the first time bows down upon his knees
and prays, "Oh! Christ, come unto me, reveal
Thyself to me, make me to know Thee, that I
may receive Thee, make me to be obedient that I
may take Thee into my life," then that man has
claimed his manhood.   I beg you, I implore you,
I adjure you that, if you be not ready to be
Christian, you at least will know that the Christian life is the only true human life, and that the
man who becomes thoroughly a Christian sets his
face toward the fulfilment of his humanity, and
so for the first time truly is a man.

March 18.

When a man turns away from his sins and enters into energetic holiness, when a man sacrifices
his own self-indulgence and goes forth a pure
servant of his God and his fellow-men, there is
only one cry in the whole gospel of that man,
and that is the cry of freedom.

March 19.

The whole sum of this title of life is service. Service to others and not to self. Self is a narrow space. I wish to speak to the young men who have just opened the door of life and to the old men who are just before the door that opens to a life beyond. Life is not an existence for self. It is this service that is the grand exponent of a successful life. To determine what success a life may attain is to see how much a life may accomplish for the bettering of humanity.

March 20.

He who understands life deeply and fully, understands life truly; he has forever renewed his life; and if there comes into our hearts, in the life which we are living, a perpetual sense that life needs renewal, a richening and refreshing, then it is in order that we may go down into the depths and see what lies at the root of things— things that we are perpetually doing and think-

6

ing.   It is that we may open to ourselves some
newer, higher life.   It is that we may understand
the life that we may live, alongside of and as a
richer devlopment of that life which we are living
from day to day, which we have been living during
the years of our life.

March 21.

Liberty is the fullest opportunity for man to be
and do the very best that is possible for him.

March 22.

What is a liberal faith, my friends?   It seems
to me that by every true meaning of the word,
by every true thought of the idea, a liberal faith
is a faith that believes much, and not a faith that
believes little.   The more a man believes, the more
liberally he exercises his capacity of faith, the
more he sends forth his intelligence into the
mysteries of God, the more he understands those
things which God chooses to reveal to his creatures, the more liberally he believes.

March 23.

Let us know ourselves children of God, and claim the liberty which God has given to every one of his children who will take it.   God bless you and give some of you, help some of us to claim, as we have never claimed before, that freedom with which the Son makes free !

March 24.

I believe in God with all my soul, because this world is inexplicable without Him and explicable with Him, and because Jesus Christ believed in Him ; and it was Jesus Christ that showed me that this world demanded God and was inexplicable without Him ; that made certain every suspicion and dream that I had had before, and Jesus Christ believed in Him.   Shall I go to the expert about chemistry or geology and ask him the truth with regard to the structure of the world and the meaning of its atoms and forces?   And shall not I go to the spiritual expert, to Him in

whom the spiritual life of man has been clearest,
and say, "O Christ, tell me what is the centre
and source and end of all?" When he says,
"God," shall ᵀ not believe Him?

March 25.

The man who lives in God knows no life except the life of God.

March 26.

Can I, can you, have Christ in human history,
Christ in the world, and live as if He were not
here? Will you not give yourself to that of Him
which you know to day? Will you not at least
lay hold of the very skirts of His garment and
say, "I see that Thou art good, I see that Thou
art true. Lead me into the goodness and truth
which by communion and sympathy shall know
Thee more. I would enter into Thee, to see
whether it has indeed come in Thee, and Thou
shalt lead me, Thou shalt teach me. Lord, I be-

lieve. I have not grasped Thee. No man has grasped Thee. The man who says that he has grasped Thee proves thereby that he does not know Thee. I know that I have not grasped Thee, but I will follow Thee, by doing righteousness, by serving truth, by knowing and acknowledging Thee until all of that shall become clear to me. I will follow Thee, and Thou shalt lead me into the glory which Thou Thyself abidest in.

March 27.

It is true, indeed, that as soon as a man becomes eager for belief, for the truth of God and for the mysteries with which God's universe is filled, he becomes all the more critical and careful. He will not any longer, if he were before, be simply greedy of things to believe, so that if any superstition comes offering itself to him he will not gather it in indiscriminately and believe it without evidence, without examination. He becomes all the more critical and careful, the more he becomes assured that belief, and not unbelief, is the true condition of his life.

March 28.

It belongs to Christ in men first to prove that man may be a Christian and yet do business ; and, in the second place, to show how a man, as he becomes a greater Christian, shall purify and lift the business that he does and make it the worthy occupation of the Son of God.

March 29.

You have got to know that religion, the service of Christ, is not something to be taken in in addition to your life ; it is your life. It is not a ribbon that you shall tie in your hat, and go down the street declaring yourself that you have accepted something in addition to the life which your fellow-men are living. It is something which, taken in your heart, shall glow in every action, so that your fellow-men shall say, " Lo, how he lives! What new life has come into him? It is that insistance upon the great essentialness of the religious life—it is the insistence that religion is not a lot of things that a man does, but is a new life that a man lives, uttering itself in new actions because it is the new life.

March 30.

Jesus the soul must have, the one yesterday, to-day and forever; He that is and was and is to be.

March 31.

Men dwell upon what He was, and upon what He is; I rather think to-day of what He is to be. And when I see men looking to the future and not to the past—nay, looking to the future and not to the present, valuing the present only as it is the seed-ground of the future, the foundation upon which the structure is to rise whose pinnacle shall some day pierce the sky—I want to tell them of the Jesus that shall be. In fuller comprehen-

sion of Him, with deeper understanding of His
life, with a more entire impression of what He is
and of what He may be to the soul, so men shall
understand Him in the days to be, and yet He
shall be the same Christ still. The future belongs
to Jesus Christ—yes, the same Christ that I believe in, and that I call upon you to believe in.
to-day, but a larger, fuller, more completely comprehended Christ—the Christ that is to be, the
same Christ that was and suffered.

April 1.

There is one great figure, and it has taken in
all Christian consciousness, that again and again
this work with Christ has been asserted to be the
true service in the army of a great master, of a
great captain, who goes before us to his victory,
that it is asserted that in that captain, in the entrance into His army, every power is set free.

April 2.

Claim your freedom in service.

April 3.

Come into the Church of Jesus Christ. There is no other body on the face of the earth that represents what she represents—the noble destiny of the human soul, the great capacity of human faith, the inexhaustible and unutterable love of God, the Christ, who stands to manifest them all.

April 4.

Are you and I going to be such creatures of our senses that we shall not believe that there are powers that touch us that we cannot see? Am I going to be so bound down to these poor fingers and to these poor eyes that I shall know myself in no larger connection with the great, unseen world? I will not. No great man, no manly man, has ever allowed such a limitation of himself. There is the unseen presence in the midst of our life, and he who will feel it may feel it, and that unseen presence speaks to him continually.

April 5.

When you sin, my friends, it is a man that sins, and a man is a child of God; and for a child of God to sin is an awful thing, not simply for the stain that he brings into the divine nature that is in him, but for the life from which it shuts him out, for the liberty which he abandons, for the enthrallment which it lays upon the soul.

April 6.

If there were any stirring in our souls after the deeper and diviner desires, could we, would we, have been satisfied until we had found Jesus, and entered into some sympathy with His life, that He might give to us what revelation of life and what guidance of will it might be possible should come from Him to men who trusted Him, until we had entered into sympathy with Him and the fascinations of His character? That is the Christian life, my friends, the thing we make so vague and mysterious and difficult.

April 7.

The most awful thought that comes to a man sometimes, is the thought of a soul that he injured years and years ago, and that he cannot find and cannot reach and cannot touch and cannot help. His own life is under better influence; his own life is uplifted; but where is the man, where is the woman, to whom he did the harm years and years ago? God save us from that. It would be hopeless if it had not the infinite hope in the endless love of God to fall back upon.

April 8.

Be happy in your faith. Be calm in your faith. Be strong with the great assurance which is in the heart of God, who knows the sorrow of our human life as none of us have ever begun to know it, and yet keeps, in the depths of His divinity, His perfect joy. Dare to be happy, even in this stricken, burdened world, because it is God's world. It is only a little while, it is only a few years, and then comes the increased work that lies beyond. Shall it be our work?

April 9.

Every man may go about his daily task with his hand clasped in the very hand of Jesus. Every man may lift up his eyes every morning and give the day that he is beginning to live to Jesus Christ, who shall fill it all with Himself. Every man may fulfill his own life into a fullness which goes beyond any possible conception that he can form of it in his own heart—different from the life of every other man that ever lived, because it is singular, individual, original and new. Every man may know the Father with the child's true heart.

April 10.

The tendency that reaches through all the regions of thought and of action; that is filling all our schools and colleges, and making them burst their bounds; that is distracting statesmen and making them wonder how their poor plans can keep pace with the great designs which are moving in the world,—is it not this: that the things which have been called the portion of the few shall more and more, and at last wholly, be the possession of every man who in his own true way will seek for their possession? The great democracy, the belief that man as man has a right to the privileges of his manhood; that they are not confined to some little select few, of peculiar nature, of peculiar education, nor by them to be distributed with niggardly hand to those who will not be content at all without them; but that they are the possession of all mankind by right; that what man can be, what it is the nature of man in this world to be, man may be; and that it is in the nature of man in this world to be higher than he is and to come to loftier conditions than those which he has dared to know,—is not that the great principle that is to-day pervading and changing all human life?

April 11.

The poet pictures to us in his imagination those things which do not appeal to our life, because they find nothing to correspond to their high portraits, to show those transformations of nature into something that is entirely different and foreign to itself. If religion be simply the dream that some men hold it to be, if it simply be the cheating of man's soul with that which has no reality to correspond to it, then it will be no more than this. Is there any assurance that is given to us, that is before the soul of man, of some great new life which it is given for man to seek, without which it is given for no man to be satisfied? I do not know where any man could find that assurance absolutely and entirely, unless there had stood forth before us the person of Him who spoke these words and who manifested them in His life. And therefore it is that, having pictured to you the richness of the life which is open to every man, his own true life, the large freedom into which he may go if, giving up his sins he enters into the fulness of the life of God.

April 12

How is it in religion? Have you not come to believe, are you not working continually upon the belief, that those great experiences, those lofty communions with God, those enterings into the secret places of His presence, that sense of oneness with His Spirit, which men used to ascribe to special natures, consecrated to a peculiar sainthood, belong to every man, everywhere, simply in virtue of his humanity; and that in some way those things may yet become the possession of every human soul; that, not only to saints who sit upon the mountain tops, in rapt psalm-singing, not merely to the souls who plunge into the deepest of overwhelming thoughts and hide themselves in the darkness which lies below the hard tread of man, but to every man may come,—and marvelous it seems when we say it,—to every man

may come the daily recognized communion with
God.

April 13.

That great thing you and I are called upon to
do—the total acceptance by our nature of the
will of God, the total acceptance by our nature of
the mastery of Jesus Christ.

April 14.

What is the great cry, what is the great aspira-
tion? As the Apostle has lifted up his voice and
sung out for us in the wondrous music of his great
epistle : "Till we all come, in the unity of the
faith, and of the knowledge of the Son of God,"
—not to some strange, unnatural thing, not to
humanity improved and changed into something
else, but till we come "to the perfect man." It
is good for us, it is right for us, it is true for us,
it makes us strong, to know that. I am struggling
toward myself, and just so far as the Christ comes
and fills me I am the thing I am, the thing I was

first of all in the thought of God, before He sent me on the earth—the thing which by His grace I shall be as eternity perfects my life in Him.

April 15.

Dear friends, dear brethren, it is not simply that you shall warm one another by the contact of your lives; it is not merely that you shall do the things which some conception of duty on your part obliges you to do; but it is that you shall have the mind of Jesus Christ, shall have in yourselves the life, and then the power of the life will show itself.

April 16.

It is the Christian life that must lie behind all enthusiasm, behind all energy; and he who would make himself or his brethren more enthusiastic, more energetic, must go behind the outward manifestations and find the source of inspiration in the controlling mind of Jesus Christ.

7

April 17.

"I am my best for the sake of all mankind."
Make that your rule in life, dear friend, and do
you not see what a calm, strong, even and completed life it brings? The world claims for you,
and your own soul claims for you, your best. It
is an obligation to yourself and an obligation to
the world. You know how little you are thinking, how little you are doing, to fulfil the best
meaning of this human life that lies before you.
Go forth and serve the world, and you will know
that you must be a nobler man in order that you
may serve it fully.

April 18.

We all know how it is, all along, with the life
in which we are living. Sometimes the sky which
is above us, which is always radiant with light,
opens its supremest depths and lets us see, as it
were, into the very city of the throne of God.
Sometimes, as we sail on the ocean, some peculiar

radiance upon its surface seems to open all its depths and let us see how deeply it mirrows all the world. So it is in the life of men, and so it is especially in the life of the great Man who stands as our Example, our Saviour, our Guide.

We never see so deeply into the depths of any human nature as when we see that nature lifting itself up by prayer. Prayer is the consummation of the human life, and it is also its spontaneous action. And so, when one prays in the presence of his fellow-men, it seems as if those fellow men, looking into his life most deeply, would be able, at any time, to enter into the richness of his consciousness, his communion with God, which must be the fulness of his life. And so we can see that when Christ stood before His disciples and offered up His heart to God, then most deeply did men look into His soul and understand Him.

April 19.

The great thing is you must live near to God. You must let no problem interest you that does not bring you into the life of God.   And remember what we talk about when we talk about coming near to God, and God coming near to us.   I do not know what it is for God to come near to us.   He is infinitely near at every moment of our life.   I do not know how He can come any nearer to me, or how I can come any nearer to Him, except in the discovery of His nearness to me. There is no coming nearer of God to man, except the showing to man how near He is to man already. And there is no coming near of man to God, except in the man's coming to know how near he always has been to the heavenly Father.   And so the coming near to God is just the opening of the eyes, just the knowing of the fact that God is infinitely near to you.   You cannot picture greater nearness.   You cannot crowd yourself to His bosom more closely than He is holding you to His bosom now.

April 20.

I am to serve my fellow-men because they are

God's children ; because, in the great, deep mystery of the words that Jesus spoke, when I am serving them I am serving Him. The life that I am to cultivate lies in Him.

April 21.

Self-culture and self-sacrifice, both present themselves as true and pressing duties of a human existence. No man has any right to contemplate the life before him, no man has any right to be living at any moment of his life, unless he knows himself to be doing all that he can to develop his soul and make it shine with its peculiar lustre in the firmament of existence. And no man has a right to be living at any moment unless he is also casting himself away and entering into the complete and devoted service of his fellow-men. Self-culture and self-sacrifice,—these two have been the great inspiring forces of existence in all ages, in every land.

April 22.

Revelation is salvation. Open your eyes and
see how close He is to your human nature, and
then you find illuminated before you the purpose
of your own self-culture, the purpose of your self-
sacrifice, and make them one.

And never think, oh, brethren, never think that
coming near to God is a terrible thing. Never
think that it is a thing to overwhelm a man with
fear and distress.

April 23.

Every duty, every will of God, every commandment of Christ, every self-surrender that a man is
called upon to obey or to make—do not think of
it as if it were simply a restraint to liberty, but
think of it as the very means of freedom, by which
we realize the very purpose of God and the fulfilment of our life.

April 24.

Oh, my friends, what does it mean to know that,
from the day the first man, in his pure rudimen-

tary innocence, trod upon this earth until to-day, when the sons of men go staggering under the burden of these thousands of years of experience, when men grow dark with the problems and bright with the joys of life,—to know that, save for Him who stands upon the hill-top of our humanity, glorifying and perfecting our humanity with His divine life, there never yet has been, in perfectness, the thing that we call man upon the earth?

April 25.

As soon as I can feel about my friend, who has become a better man, that he has become a larger and not a smaller, a freer and not a more imprisoned man, as soon as I lift up my voice and say that the man is free, then I understand him more fully, and he becomes a revelation to me in the higher and richer life which is possible for me to live.

April 26.

I am anxious to have you know that to be a

Christian does not mean primarily to believe this or that. It does not mean primarily, although it means necessarily afterward, to do this or that. But it means to know the presence of a true personal Christ among us and to follow Him. Here is the only true power by which a religion can become perpetual.

April 27.

I know not what our Christian faith means unless these things are true, unless it be true that behind all enthusiasm and energy must be the deep life of the soul opening itself to God, and that the soul, opening itself to God and filled with Him, becomes by the possession of God its own true self, recognizes this as its own natural condition, and sees how unmanly and unnatural is any other way of liv'ng.

April 28.

And so it must certainly be true, somehow or other, that self-culture and self-sacrifice are not

merely capable of being reconciled to one another
by compromises which they shall make between
them, but that they are mutual ministers to one another, and that the more truly a man sacrifices himself to others, the more truly shall he live in his own
life ; the more truly he lives in his own life, the
more truly shall he be a sacrifice to his fellow men.

April 29.

It does not take a great man to do great things
It only takes a consecrated, a devoted man ; be
cause God does everything, and man does nothing
except what God does through him.

April 30.

And don't dare to hurt any soul ; for to hurt a
soul is to touch the very substance of the life of
God.

May 1.

In all the simplest characters that line between
the mental and moral natures is always vague and

indistinct.   They run together, and in their best combinations you are unable to discriminate, in the wisdom which is their result, how much is moral and how much is intellectual.   You are unable to tell whether in the wise acts and words which issue from such a life there is more of the right-eousness that comes of a clear conscience, or of the sagacity that comes of a clear brain.

May 2.

The essence of the Christian life—what is it but the perfecting of the human life by the in-dwelling of the Spirit of the Lord Jesus Christ?

May 3.

I wish I had the power to convince every one of my hearers of the importance of service.   In service you throw yourself into another life.   The other life becomes part of yourself, you part of that other life ; you are one.   You work together for the bettering of the world.   Just so you enter into God and the divine life enters into you.

You do not surrender to pope, priest, or church, but still have your own independence. You simply surrender to God.

May 4

May Christ be with you, may you be with Him, every day, every hour!

May 5.

Let the heart be right, and the voice will shout and the hands must work.

May 6.

Do whatever you can to help every struggling soul, to add new strength to any staggering cause, the poor sick man that is by you, the poor wronged man whom you with your influence might vindicate, the poor boy in your shop that you may set with new hope upon the road of life that is beginning already to look dark to him. I cannot tell you what it is. You know your duty. No man ever looked for it and did not find it.

May 7.

There is only One to whose words we can turn to seek our guidance and direction, our inspiration and our joy.

May 8.

As man has been, so has the world responded to his touch and call.

May 9.

Into every soul, just so far and just so fast as it is possible for that soul to receive it, God beats His life and gives His help.

May 10.

The man of the nineteenth century thinks very differently from the man of the eighteenth, but the love with which he worships God is the same love. The evangelical has different dogmas from the old Georgian Churchman, but they bow before the same mercy seat, and resist the same temptations by the same grace.

May 11.

I will put my life into the Church ; all the more I will drink the strength that she can give to me.

May 12.

Every man who is a Christian must live a Christian life that is peculiarly his own.

May 13.

God will make you good by sending His light and love into that past of yours and giving all that there is good in its true development and consecration.

May 14.

When shall we learn that with all true men it is not what they intend to do, but it is what the qualities of their natures bind them to do, that determines their career ?

May 15.

The life which is lived under the inspiration of

Jesus Christ, and which we call the Christian life, is the freest of all lives, because it is the highest.

May 16.

The study of human progress is one of the strangest studies in which we can engage. When we look about us, we see the one-sided fashion in which the world advances, now throwing forward one side, and then advancing the other side until it shall come up to it. It is not thus that the highest progress of the soul is pictured. It is not by putting forth first one part of our nature, to the exclusion of the other parts, and then letting the other parts overtake it, that man is really to advance. There must be a great power of advance that shall go on along the whole line. It must be that the total man, with all the powers of his existence, with all the life that has been given to him to live, shall move on together. That is the progress that we expect in the clear atmosphere, in the pure life, of the eternal world.

May 17.

Never fear to bring the sublimest comfort to the smallest trouble.

May 18.

Do not dare to think ever that you, you who go with the consecrated soul to seek your brother, are the power by which that soul is being sought in the universe of God. God loves every soul to which you go, with a love that your love toward Him cannot begin to understand. God is seeking every soul that you are seeking, with the immediate impulses of His grace and love, in ways too deep and mysterious for you and me to begin to comprehend. That will not make us think, in one slightest degree, that our seeking of that soul is useless; but it will make us go with great eagerness and with faith and with hope, doing what we can for every brother, but thankful to know that that brother is God's child, and that He is seeking that soul and ministering His love to it directly, as well as though the feeble ministry that we can bring.

May 19.

Come near to God with the deep sense of how near God wants you to come to Him. Open your eyes and see God, with the certainty that when they open, they shall see upon His face the infinite love and the divine patience with which He is waiting for your soul.

May 20.

What will heaven be? What will be the substance on which they shall stand who worship God and praise Him in the ages of eternity? I find manifold fitness in the answer that tells us that it shall be a "sea of glass mingled with fire." Heaven will not be pure stagnation, not idleness, not any more luxurious dreaming over the spiritual repose that has been safely and forever won; but active, tireless, earnest work; fresh, live enthusiasm for the high labors which eternity will offer. These vivid inspirations will play through our deep repose, and make it more mighty in the service of God than any feverish and unsatisfied toil of earth has ever been. The sea of glass will be mingled with fire. Here too we have the type and standard of that heavenliness of character which ought to be ripening in all of us now, as we are getting ready for that spiritual life.

May 21.

Dreadful will be the day when the world becomes contented, when one great universal satisfaction spreads itself over the world. Sad will be the day for every man when he becomes absolutely contented with the life that he is living, with the thoughts that he is thinking, with the deeds that he is doing, when there is not forever beating at the doors of his soul some great desire to do something larger which he knows that he was meant and made to do because he is a child of God.

8

May 22.

Do not think that greatness and vigor of interest involve fury and he.t. Be calm. Go to your fellow-man and invite him to come and live the life in Jesus Christ, as if you were inviting him to do the most natural thing that it is possible for him to do; as if you were bidding him to come and be himself. Be calm; for calmness harmonizes the tumultuous elements of existence in the consciousness of God. Be your best, for the good of God's children.

May 23.

What a man comes to be when he becomes a Christian is a deeper, truer, more entire, more essential man. When the great ocean beats and gurgles over the reef that stands across the bay, and pours itself in upon the inlet which is a real part of its own life, the inlet shakes and trembles with the incoming of the sea; but by and by it

knows that thus, and thus only, has it come to be
what it was made to be.

May 24.

Let no man preach to you any doctrine which
would come in conflict with the fullest development of the power of your life. Every power is
to be brought into its fullest development. You
are to make body, soul and spirit just as full and
united, as they are bound together in your personal existence, as you can. And you are to
serve your fellow-men with the fullest consecration of your life; but you can do this only as you
serve, through yourself and through your brethren,
the God whose children you and those brethren are.

May 25.

There are certain experiences in every life
which have their power just in this, that they
break through the elaborate surface, and get down
to the simplest thoughts and emotions of the

human heart. Great sickness, sudden bereave-
ment, great joy, intense love or enthusiasm,
fatherhood, the near sight of death, - all of these
supreme experiences of life are characterized by
the breadth, the largeness of the simple thoughts
and feelings they awaken. In them you have
the crust broken to fragments, and the great
heart of life laid open. And if that heart, laid
open, is inevitably, universally spiritual; if, as we
always see in these supreme moments of the life,
a soul most vividly asserts itself, the man insists upon another world and on a God.

May 26.

The man never lived, save He who perfected
our humanity, who ever did the very best he
could. You dishonor your life, you not simply
shut your eyes to certain facts, you not simply say
an infinitely absurd and foolish thing, but you
dishonor your human life if you say that you have
done in any day of your life, or in all the days of

your life put together, the very best that you
could, or been the very best man that you could
be. You! what are you? Again I say, The
child of God; and this which you have been,
what is it? Look over it, see how selfish it has
been, see how material it has been, how it has
lived in the depths when it might have lived on
the heights; see how it has lived in the little,
narrow range of selfishness, when it might have
been as broad as all humanity—nay, when it
might have been as the God of humanity.

May 27.

The very moment I become conscious of my
own individual existence, I also become conscious
of this vast ocean of existence beating in upon
me from every side, through every avenue of ap-
proach, meeting my gaze in every direction in
which I look toward the horizon that sweeps
around me, and pressing upon me through the
lives with which I am surrounded.

May 28.

It would be intolerable to us if we could not trace tendencies in our life. If everything stood still, or if things only moved around in a circle, it would be a dreary and a dreadful thing to live. But we rejoice in life because it seems to be carrying us somewhere, because its darkness seems to be rolling on towards light, and even its pain to be moving onward to a hidden joy. We bear with incompleteness because of the completion which is prophesied and hoped for.

May 29.

The forgiveness of our sins, the separation from the circumstances of our sins, the removal from our temptations, everything that the Lord can do for us, are but leading on to this, that He shall fill us with Himself, that we shall make our lives the very utterance of His life and of the life of the Father, that comes to us from Him.

May 30.

We moralize, we philosophize, about the discontent of man. We give little reasons for it; but the real reason of it all is—this, that which everything lying behind it really signifies, that man is greater than his circumstances, and that God is always calling to him to come up to the fulness of his life.

May 31.

The world, as it goes on, is to become vastly more individualistic than it has ever been yet. Every soul is to feel the awful sweetness of being commissioned by God to live, and of being different from every other life.

June 1.

The noble souls have always known the necessity that nature has laid upon them, in all ages, to develop their souls by self culture and self sacrifice. If study, in which men have meditated upon the problems of their own life, has set men fighting their own personal battles, wrestling with their own personal sins, self-sacrifice also has set up its altars in the world.   It has taught men, in the darkest ages, to live not only for themselves, but for others.   It has taught men to know that the noblest thing men could do with human life was to give that human life away.   If self-culture has built the schools, self-sacrifice has built the altars, has sent men to their martyrdom, has made men ingenious and gracious, as they have struggled with the problems of their own existence.   It is impossible for us not to recognize both of these as the two great missions, the two great intuitions, the two great fields of duty, which God has offered to every man.

June 2.

I cannot help calling you now to think about Him who gives, not merely by His words, but by the whole of His own person and life, that manifestation of the reality of the divine existence and tempts us to follow after Him. In other words, we come to-day to think of Christ, Christ who claims to be the master of the world. Christ from whom the revelation of that higher life has come. * * * * It is our Christ in whom we Christians believe. It is the Christ in whom a great many of you listening to me now claim to believe—I do myself—in whom many of you do believe, whom many of you have followed into that newer life. I would to God that I could so set Him before you to-day, could so make you feel his actual presence in the life which we are living, which we may be living, that there should be no question in any man of the power that is open before him to enter into the higher life and to fulfil his soul to God.

June 3.

It is the very abundance of the strange speculations with regard to Christ, it is the very strangeness of the theories that have been formed with regard to Him, that has shown me how He has drawn the hearts of men, how He has not let them go, but compelled them to fasten themselves to Him, to think about Him and try to follow Him in such poor, blind ways as they were able to give themselves to Him in. This, then, is the Christian faith. This is the way in which the larger life opens before mankind, by the following of a person, by the giving of the life into the dominion and the guidance and the obedience of one who goes forward into that life, himself thoroughly believing in it—for Jesus believed in it with all His human soul.

June 4.

You are to cultivate yourself for the sake of your fellow-men, and you are to serve your fellow-men for the sake of your own self-culture.

June 5.

Let me know Christ, let me be Christ's ; then

shall come the enthusiasm without my trying to lift up my voice; then shall come the energy without my even stretching out my hand.

June 6.

What is it that has happened to you, my Christian friend, my Christian brother, in these days in which your whole soul rejoices? You have been filled with Christ, you have been lifted up into a union with Him, that beats with the beating of His heart, shines with the impulse and enthusiam of His desires. What has happened to you? Are you less a man than you used to be? Has your manhood been destroyed, and some strange, unknown thing put in its place? Do those of your brethren who are around you look at you and wonder how you have become so, how you have undergone that astonishing change? Nay, in every step which you take, in every word that you speak, in every touch of your life upon every other life, do not you and

those around you know that you have come a
little nearer,—not yet to the fulfillment, but a
little nearer—to the wondrous thing which it is
to be a man ?

June 7.

" Is it right that a man should entirely sacrifice
himself to his fellow-men ? Is it right that a
man should give away his life in order that his
brethren may be saved ? " We see it in many
ways, with a thousand meanings—that vast truth ;
but when we carry it on to its fullest interpreta-
tion, it is an awful doctrine, a doctrine that it is
inconceivable that God should teach His children.
God can never really sacrifice the essential fulfilment of any life to the service which it could
render to any other life. Much I may be called
upon to give up, much I may be called upon to
surrender. I may surrender my comfort, my
means, my time, my cultivation. But myself I
have no right to give entirely to any man. to give
for the growth of my fellow-men. God never

can ask a man to give his own true life, his own
real self, his own essential and absolute self, the
fulness of his own life, even for the salvation of
the world. It is the story of the great man's
life; it was the story of the divine life of Jesus.
He gave Himself absolutely for man, but He
never gave Himself away to man. He never
sacrificed that which belonged to His Father.

June 8.

Why am I to cultivate myself? Simply that I
may make this knowledge of myself the most
complete of all the things here on earth, as perfect as I can? Why am I to serve my fellow-
men? Because I would help them a little in the
struggles which would lift them toward God?
Both of them are reasons; but both lie within
the one great reason which exists in the mystery
of the union of all men, and the existence of all
life, in God. I am to serve myself, I am to
educate myself, because I am a part of God, be-

cause I am fulfilling this life, which is a part of God's life.

June 9.

It is true of every great nature which in its development finds some difficulties, some obscurities, some anomalies, that it is to escape from those obscurities and difficulties only by making itself greater, and not by making itself less.

June 10.

I understand perfectly well the stories which men tell us of the tremendous struggle that has shaken them, body and soul. If only they could come into the presence of their Father ! But I know that no such struggle is a necessary experience of the human life. I know that the great life of man, coming near to God, is meant to be the most natural fulfilment of his human existence. I will think no man's experience an unnatural one, because it has not been shaken by terrors and by fears. I know that the experience which pictures all our experience, opened, under the skies of Nazareth and on the sweet waters of the Lake of Galilee, peacefully and calmly into the perfect knowledge that He and the Father were absolutely one.

June 11.

"Aye, but sin!" you say. Yes, sin. And so it may be that through jungles and through briers and morasses you must find your way to Him. But let not your eye be upon the jungle under your feet, but upon the certain light that shines beyond.

June 12.

Men have recognized that word of Christ, and found the fulfilment of it in their own lives; and that has been the Christian religion,—just exactly what it was in the old days when Jesus was present in Jerusalem and Galilee. Just exactly what men did then, men have been doing in all the generations that have come since. Just exactly what was possible then is possible for them now—that we may become the followers of that same Christ and the receivers through Him of the divine life, by which alone the human life is perfected and fulfilled.

June 13.

Come home and strive for greater nobleness, and the bond between your human life and other human lives will call you forth again and show you how large a part of your fulfilment lies in other natures.

June 14.

Shall I sit down in my study and say, "I am to make myself the very best man, the fullest man that I possibly can, in order that I may do some work with myself by and by?" On the other hand, shall I go out to my dealings with the world, and serve my fellow-men, in order that I may serve myself?"

We must come back to our Lord again, and everything becomes clear in that very clearest life which is our perpetual inspiration and study. Christ was cultivating Jesus of Nazareth, and yet was remembering the fellow-men who were around him in Jerusalem and Galilee. But all this was subject to and governed by His entire consecration to His God.

June 15.

I shall find the fellow-men whom I served, when I look forth, not simply into their pinched and haggard faces here on the street, not simply into the social conditions under which I see them laboring, but when I see them in the idea of their existence, and think of them and all people as comprehended in and forming part of the existence of God.

June 16.

We crave freedom. We believe that only in freedom will mankind fulfil its best life. But freedom immediately brings its difficulties. its contradictions, its disturbances, where before everything has seemed to be consistency and

9

peace.   How shall we escape from the dangers of
liberty?   Shall it be by restricting liberty? No,
but by increasing liberty. So mankind shall learn
to escape the dangers of liberty only by making
man more free.   The dangers of liberty are only
to be overcome when it has reached a stage
higher than any partial development which it has
yet attained—when it has reached it full and
glorious development.

June 17.

The great richness of nature, the great richness
of life, comes when we understand that behind
every specific action of man there is some one
of the more elemental and primary forces of the
universe that are always trying to express themselves.

June 18.

Self-culture is going to escape from the dangers
of self-culture only by becoming a deeper power
of self-culture, and self-sacrifice is going to escape

from its dangers only by sacrificing itself more completely. In order to cultivate himself more completely the man is to sacrifice himself more completely. In order to sacrifice himself more completely, he is to cultivate himself more completely. These two great principles of existence will only come into harmony with one another in mutually ministering to one another, as they pour themselves out together and mingle with one another, and find themselves a part of the great plan of God.

June 19.

I do some work for my fellow-men to-day, and I am a better fulfilment of the purpose that God had in my existence; I come to a fuller completion of myself; I am fitter for some of the work that this great, hungry, needy, crying world demands.

June 20.

I know that there is no greater conception of any great fact in this world which man can know to be true, which he does not know by that higher faculty of faith. Ah, faith! the word that we dishonor, the word that really is the glory of our life—"the substance of things hoped for, the evidence of things not seen."

June 21.

I dare to believe that there are young men who, failing to be touched by every promise of their own salvation and every threatening of their own damnation, will still lift themselves up and take upon them the duty of men, and be soldiers of Jesus Christ, and have a part in the battle, and have a part somewhere in the victory that is sure to come. Don't be selfish anywhere. Don't be selfish, most of all, in your religion. Let yourselves free into your religion, and be utterly unselfish.

June 22.

The soul that trifles and toys with self-sacrifice never can get its true joy and power. Only the soul that, with an overwhelming impulse and a perfect trust, gives itself up forever to the life of other men, finds the delight and peace which such complete self-surrender has to give.

June 23.

Oh, seek independence. Insist upon independence. Insist that you will not be the slave of the poor, petty standards of your fellow-men. But insist upon it only in the way in which it can be insisted upon, by becoming absolutely the servant of their needs.

June 24.

Jesus Christ comes to us in the noblest part of our nature, and claims us there for our true life within Himself.

June 25.

Because you must worship, therefore you must have God.

June 26.

Let us come under the inspiration of Jesus Christ Himself, who says to us, in these words which we have repeatedly read to one another, that it is the truth that is to make us free, and that the entrance of the man therefore into that freedom is the largest freedom of every region of man's life.

June 27.

I want to claim, that which I believe with all my soul, that he who lives in the faith of Jesus Christ lives in the freest action of his mental powers, and there sees before him and makes himself a part of the large world into which man shall enter, in which he has perfect liberty and can exercise his powers as he could never have exercised them without.

June 28.

The only way to be sure that God gave us our physical life is to let Him give us the spiritual life which shall declare for the physical life an adequate and worthy purpose.

June 29.

Christ can give the world the thing it needs in unknown ways and methods that we have not yet begun to suspect.

June 30.

Read your own nature deeper and you will understand your Christ. * * * God bless you and go with you wherever you go. Speak great things, but know that many things that the world calls little are great things. To so live and at the end to know, or not to know, that one soul in God's world is better for our having lived,—that is enough.

DAILY THOUGHTS

FROM

HENRY DRUMMOND, F.R.S.E., F.G.S.

WITH A

BIOGRAPHICAL SKETCH.

BALTIMORE:
R. H. WOODWARD & COMPANY.

BIOGRAPHICAL SKETCH.

BIOGRAPHICAL SKETCH

OF

HENRY DRUMMOND, F.R.S.E., F.G.S.

———

PROFESSOR DRUMMOND was born in Stirling, Scotland, in the year 1851. His father was a justice of the peace. At an early age he developed a desire for serious study, and after some preparation in the schools, at home, he was sent to the University of Edinburgh, and afterwards to Tubingen, Germany. At both places, his rare gifts marked him out among his classmates as a young man of especial promise. Having determined on a ministerial career, he passed through the Free Church Divinity Hall, and after his ordination was appointed to a mission-station at

Malta.   Here he employed his leisure in the pursuit of his favorite studies, Theology and Science, boldly grappling with the problems presented by the most recent researches and developments of the latter in the effort to seek a reconciliation with the spirit and essence of the former.

The result of these studies was made apparent when, on his return to Scotland in 1877, the brilliant young man, barely twenty-six years of age, was appointed Lecturer in Science at the Free Church College in Glasgow.   It was yet more apparent when, in 1883, the free fruition of his thought and experience was presented to the world in a remarkable book entitled " Natural Laws in the Spiritual World."   This book might be looked upon as in some sort an amplification of the theme which Tennyson also had chosen in that magnificent though illy-named poem, " The Higher Pantheism," and might have taken for its text the pregnant line,

And if God thunders by law, the thunder is still His voice.

The book was at once received with great favor. It was republished in America. It was translated into French, German, Dutch and Norwegian. He became Professor of Science in the Free Church College in 1884.

In 1889 he was invited to make an address at Moody's College at Oxford. This address was entitled, "The Greatest Thing in the World." Its publication in book form was instantly demanded. Slight as was the pamphlet in bulk, its success more than repeated the success of his first literary effort. Nearly a quarter of a million copies were sold in Great Britain alone. It is significant of the author's modesty, self-restraint and singleness of mind that while the public is clamoring for every line he may choose to give them he withholds the manuscript of numerous addresses, spoken but never printed, and that his published books represent only the merest fraction of his intellectual life-work.

Prof. Drummond has a singular union of gifts.

As a rule, the glory of the orator is one thing, and the glory of the writer is another. Prof. Drummond is one of the few brilliant exceptions to that rule. How often do we find the impassioned sentences of the orator turn cold and lifeless in the printed page! How often does the brilliant writer seem stilted and unnatural in spoken word!

Judged as a writer, he has command of a vigorous, nervous, flexible style. His words are simple, he loves monsyllables more than polysyllables, and Saxon more than Latin. He has a wealth of illustrations to draw upon—illustrations that are worthy of the name and do illustrate, do cast a flood of light upon his meaning. Yet these illustrations are of the homeliest sort. They are drawn from life more than from books. They are not stock figures of speech. They are the fruit of long and minute observation ;-they indicate a brain that is ever active to seize the multiple analogies presented by the world around us.

The author has thought and studied much, but he has seen more. He does not misjudge his audience. He makes no ostentatious effort to soar above them, nor is he guilty of any ostentatious condescension. He says his say in straight, honest fashion ; his rhetoric has a robust sincerity that convinces as well as thrills.

10

DAILY THOUGHTS.

July 1.

Whenever you attempt a good work you will find other men doing the same kind of work, and probably doing it better. Envy them not. Envy is a feeling of ill-will to those who are in the same line as ourselves, a spirit of covetousness and detraction. How little Christian work even is a protection against un-Christian feeling! That most despicable of all the unworthy moods which cloud a Christian's soul assuredly waits for for us on the threshold of every work, unless we are fortified with this grace of magnanimity. Only one thing truly need the Christian envy, the large, rich, generous soul which "envieth not."

July 2.

All around us Christians are wearing themselves out in trying to be better. The amount of spiritual longing in the world—in the hearts of un-numbered thousands of men and women in whom we should never suspect it; among the wise and thoughtful; among the young and gay, who seldom assuage and never betray their thirst—this is one of the most wonderful and touching facts of life.

July 3.

"Seekest thou great things for thyself?" said the prophet; "*seek them not.*" Why? Because there is no greatness in *things*. Things cannot be great. The only greatness is unselfish love.

July 4.

He that would be happy, let him remember that there is but one way—it is more blessed, it is more happy, to give than to receive.

July 5.

Do not grudge the hand that is moulding the still too shapeless image within you. It is growing more beautiful, though you see it not, and every touch of temptation may add to its perfection.

July 6.

Try to give up the idea that religion comes to us by chance, or by mystery, or by caprice. It comes to us by natural law, or by supernatural law, for all law is Divine.

July 7.

Love is not a thing of enthusiastic emotion. It is a rich, strong, manly, vigorous expression of the whole round Christian character—the Christlike nature in its fullest development. And the constituents of this great character are only to be built up by ceaseless practice.

July 8.

As memory scans the past, above and beyond all the transitory pleasures of life, there leap forward those supreme hours when you have been enabled to do unnoticed kindnesses to those round about you, things too trifling to speak about, but which you feel have entered into your eternal life.

July 9.

Who is Christ? He who fed the hungry, clothed the naked, visited the sick. And where is Christ? Where?—whoso shall receive a little child in My name receiveth Me. And who are Christ's? Every one that loveth is born of God.

July 10.

Souls are made sweet not by taking the acid fluids out, but by putting something in—a great Love, a new Spirit, the Spirit of Christ.

July 11.

To be lost is to live in an unregenerate condition, loveless and unloved, and to be saved is to love; and he that dwelleth in love dwelleth already in God. For God is Love.

July 12.

Two painters each painted a picture to illustrate his conception of rest. The first choose for his scene a still, lone lake among the far-off mountains. The second threw on his canvas a thundering water-fall, with a fragile birch tree bending over the foam; at the fork of a branch, almost wet with the cataract's spray, a robin sat on its nest. The first was only *Stagnation;* the last was *Rest*. For in Rest there are always two elements—tranquility and energy; silence and turbulence; creation and destruction; fearlessness and fearfulness. Thus it was in Christ.

July 13.

There is only one thing greater than happiness in the world, and that is holiness.

July 14.

Christ's invitation to the weary and heavy-laden is a call to begin life over again upon a new

principle—upon His own principle. "Watch
My way of doing things," He says. "Follow
Me. Take life as I take it. Be meek and lowly
and you will find Rest."

July 15.

Christianity as Christ taught is the truest phi-
losophy of life ever spoken. But let us be quite
sure when we speak of Christianity that we mean
Christ's Christianity.

July 16.

To love abundantly is to live abundantly, and
to love forever is to live forever.

July 17.

Men can be to other men as the shadow of a
great rock in a thirsty land. Much more Christ ;
much more Christ as Perfect Man ; much more
still as Saviour of the world.

July 18.

Through whatever media it reaches us, all true joy and gladness find their source in Christ.

July 19.

Christ is the source of Joy to men in the sense in which He is the source of Rest. His people share His life, and therefore share its consequences, and one of these is Joy.

July 20.

Joy lay in mere constant living in Christ's presence, with all that that implied of peace, of shelter and of love; partly in the influence of that Life upon mind and character and will; and partly in the inspiration to live and work for others, with all that that brings of self-riddance and Joy in others' gain. All these, in different ways and at different times, are sources of pure Happiness.

July 21.

You will find, if you think for a moment, that the people who influence you are people who believe in you.

July 22.

Christ saw that men took life painfully. To some it was a weariness, to others a failure, to many a tragedy, to all a struggle and a pain. How to carry this burden of life had been the whole world's problem. And here is Christ's solution: "Carry it as I do. Take life as I take it. Look at it from My point of view. Interpret it upon My principles. Take My yoke and learn of Me, and you will find it easy. For My yoke is easy, works easily, sits right upon the shoulders, and *therefore* My burden is light."

July 23.

Since we are what we are by the impacts of those who surround us, those who surround themselves with the highest will be those who change into the highest.

July 24.

The infallible receipt for Happiness is to do good ; and the infallible receipt for doing good is to abide in Christ. The surest proof that all this is a plain matter of Cause and Effect is that men may try every other conceivable way of finding Happiness, and they will fail. Only the right cause in each case can produce the right effect. There is no mystery about Happiness whatever. Put in the right ingredients and it must come out. He that abideth in Him will bring forth much fruit; and bringing forth much fruit is Happiness.

July 25.

If you love you will unconsciously fulfil the whole law.

July 26.

We all reflecting as a mirror the character of Christ are transformed into the same Image from character to character—from a poor character to a better one, from a better one to one a little better still, from that to one still more complete, until by slow degrees the Perfect Image is attained.

July 27.

To copy virtues one by one has somewhat the same effect as eradicating the vices one by one; the temporary result is an overbalanced and incongruous character.

Character is a unity, and all the virtues must advance together to make the perfect man.

July 28.

To live with Socrates—with unveiled face— must have made one wise; with Aristides, just. Francis of Assisi must have made one gentle; Savonarola, strong.   But to have lived with Christ must have made one like Christ; that is to say, *A Christian.*

July 29.

As the man is to the animal in the slowness of his evolution, so is the spiritual man to the natural man. Foundations which have to bear the weight of an eternal life must be surely laid. Character is to wear for ever; who will wonder or grudge that it cannot be developed in a day?

July 30.

A religion of effortless adoration may be a religion for an angel, but never for a man. Not in the contemplative, but in the active, lies true hope; not in rapture, but in reality, lies true life; not in the realm of ideals, but among tangible things, is man's sanctification wrought.

July 31.

The mind, the memory, the soul, is simply a vast chamber panelled with looking-glass. And upon this miraculous arrangement and "endowment depends the capacity of mortal souls to " reflect the character of the Lord."

August 1.

No man can change himself. Throughout the New Testament you will find that wherever these moral and spiritual transformations are described the verbs are in the passive. Not more certain is it that it is something outside the thermometer that produces a change in the thermometer, than it is something outside the soul of man that produces a moral change upon him.

August 2.

The kingdom of God is not going to religious meetings, and hearing strange religious experiences; the kingdom of God is doing what is right—living at peace with all men, being filled with joy in the Holy Ghost.

August 3.

The Image of Christ that is forming within

us—that is life's one charge. Let every project stand aside for that. "Till Christ be formed," no man's work is finished, no religion crowned, no life has fulfilled its end. Is the infinite task begun? When, how, are we to be different? Time cannot change men. Death cannot change men. Christ can. Wherefore *put on Christ.*

August 4.

It is for active service soldiers are drilled and trained and fed and armed. That is why you and I are in the world at all—not to prepare to go out of it some day ; but to serve God actively in it *now.*

August 5.

If my brother is short-sighted, I must not abuse him nor speak against him; I must pity him, and, if possible, try to improve his sight or to make things that he is to look at so bright that he cannot help seeing.

11

August 6.

Christ never failed to distinguish between doubt and unbelief. Doubt is *can't believe;* unbelief is *won't believe.* Doubt is honesty; unbelief is obstinacy.

August 7.

Banish for ever from your minds the idea that religion is *subtraction.* It does not tell us to give things up, but rather gives us something so much better that they give themselves up.

August 8.

Keep religion in its place, and it will take you straight through life, and straight to your Father in heaven when life is over.   *   *   *   Religion out of its place in human life is the most miserable thing in the world.   There is nothing that requires so much to be kept in its place as religion, and its place is what? second? third? "First."

August 9.

We are, of course, not responsible for everything that is said in the name of Christianity;
but a man does not give up medicine because
there are quack doctors, and no man has a right
to give up his Christianity because there are
spurious or inconsistent Christians.

August 10.

Truth is not a product of the intellect alone;
it is a product of the whole nature. * * It
would be a pity if all these problems could be
solved. The joy of the intellectual life would
be largely gone. I would not rob a man of his
problems, nor would I have another man rob me of
my problems. They are the delight of life, and
the whole intellectual world would be stale and
unprofitable if we knew everything.

August 11.

Many a man thinks he is looking at truth when

he is only looking at the spectacles he has put on to see it with.

August 12.

It will never do to exaggerate one truth at the expense of another, and a truth may be turned into a falsehood very, very easily, by simply being either too much enlarged or too much diminished.

August 13.

Your views are just what you see with your own eyes, and my views are just what I see ; and what I see depends on just where I stand, and what you see depends on just where you stand.

August 14.

If any of you want to know how to begin to be a Christian, all I can say is that you should begin to do the next thing you find to be done as Christ would have done it.

August 15.

What can be gathered on the surface as to the process of Regeneration in the individual soul? From the analogies of Biology we should expect three things: First, that the New Life should dawn suddenly; second, that it should come "without observation;" third, that it should develop gradually. On two of these points there can be little controversy. The gradualness of growth is a characteristic which strikes the simplest observer. Long before the word Evolution was coined Christ applied it in this very connection—"First the blade, then the ear, then the full corn in the ear." Growth is most gradual in the highest forms. Man attains his maturity after a score of years; the monad completes its humble cycle in a day. What wonder if development be tardy in the Creature of Eternity! A Christian's sun has sometimes set, and a critical world has seen, as yet, no corn in the ear. As yet? "As yet," in this long Life, has not begun. Grant him the years proportionate to his place in the scale of Life. "The time of harvest is *not yet.*"

August 16.

There is only one great character in the world that can really draw out all that is best in man. He is so far above all others in influencing men for good that He stands alone. That man was the founder of Christianity. To be a Christian man is to have that Character for our ideal in life, to live under its influence, to do what He would wish us to do, to live the kind of life He would have lived in our house, and had He our day's routine to go through. It would not, per-haps, alter the forms of our life, but it would alter the spirit and aims and motives of our life, and the Christian man is he who in that sense lives under the influence of Jesus Christ

August 17.

It is not worth seeking the kingdom of God unless we seek it *first.*

August 18.

Causes and effects are eternal arrangements, set in the constitution of the world ; fixed beyond man's ordering. What man can do is to place himself in the midst of a chain of sequences. Thus he can get things to grow : thus he himself can grow. But the grower is the Spirit of God.

August 19.

The test of value of the different verities of truth depends upon one thing ; whether they have or have not a sanctifying power.

August 20.

What is it that saves the life of the world from being utterly rotten, but the Christian elements that are in it ?

August 21.

Why is Love greater than faith ? Because the end is greater than the means. And why is it

greater than charity? Because the whole is
greater than the part. Love is greater than faith,
because the end is greater than the means. What
is the use of having faith? It is to connect the
soul with God. And what is the object of connecting man with God? That he may become
like God. But God is Love. Hence Faith, the
means, is in order to Love, the end.

August 22.

" Love is the fulfilling of the law." It is the
rule for fulfilling all rules, the new commandment
for keeping all the old commandments, Christ's
one secret of the Christian life.

August 23.

What a noble gift it is, the power of playing
upon the souls and wills of men, and rousing
them to lofty purposes and holy deeds. Paul
says, " If I speak with the tongues of men and
of angels, and have not love, I am become as

sounding brass, or a tinkling cymbal.'' And we
all know why. We have all felt the brazenness
of words without emotion, the hollowness, the
unaccountable unpersuasiveness, of eloquence
behind which lies no Love.

August 24.

If a truth makes a man a better man, then let
him focus upon it and get all the acquaintance
with it he can.

August 25.

The spirit of Christ was the scientific spirit.
He founded His religion upon facts; and He
asked all men to found their religion upon facts.
Now, gentlemen, get up the facts of Christianity,
and take men to the facts.

August 26.

We hear much of love to God; Christ spoke
much of love to man. We make a great deal of
peace with heaven; Christ made much of peace
on earth.

August 27.

Take into your sphere of labor, where you also mean to lay down your life, that simple charm, Love, and your life-work must succeed.

August 28.

Spiritual Life is not something outside ourselves. The idea is not that Christ is in heaven, and that we can stretch out some mysterious faculty and deal with Him there. This is the vague form in which many conceive the truth, but it is contrary to Christ's teaching and to the analogy of nature. Vegetable Life is not contained in a reservoir somewhere in the skies, and measured out spasmodically at certain seasons. The Life is *in* every plant and tree, inside its own substance and tissue, and continues there until it dies. Life is not one of the homeless forces which promiscuously inhabit space, or which can be gathered like electricity from the clouds and dissipated back again into space. Life is definite and resident; and Spiritual Life is not a visit from a force, but a resident tenant in the soul.

August 29.

It is the man who is the missionary, it is not his words.

August 30.

What do you say to a man when he says to you, "Why do you believe in miracles?" I say, "Because I have seen them." He says, "When?" I say, "Yesterday." He says, "Where?" "Down such-and-such a street I saw a man who was a drunkard redeemed by the power of an unseen Christ and saved from sin. That is a miracle." There are fifty other arguments for miracles, but none so good as that you have seen them. Perhaps you are one yourself. But take you a man and show him a miracle with his own eyes. Then he will believe.

August 31:

Where Love is, God is. He that dwelleth in

Love dwelleth in God. God is Love. Therefore *love*.

September 1.

If a man neglect himself for a few years he will change into a worse man and a lower man. If it is his body that he neglects, he will deteriorate into a wild and bestial savage—like the dehumanized men who are discovered sometimes upon desert islands. If it is his mind, it will degenerate into imbecility and madness—solitary confinement has the power to unmake men's minds and leave them idiots. If he neglect his conscience, it will run off into lawlessness and vice. Or, lastly, if it is his soul, it must inevitably atrophy, drop off in ruin and decay.

We have here, then, a thoroughly natural basis for the question before us. If we neglect, with this universal principle staring us in the face, how shall we escape? So, if we neglect the soul, how shall it escape the natural retrograde movement, the inevitable relapse into barrenness and death?

"How shall we escape if we neglect so great salvation?"—*Hebrews*.

September 2.

Have you ever noticed how much of Christ's life was spent in doing kind things—in *merely* doing kind things? Run over it with that in view, and you will find that He spent a great proportion of His time simply in making people happy, in doing good turns to people. What God *has* put in our power is the happiness of those about us, and that is largely to be secured by our being kind to them.

September 3.

Christ's life outwardly was one of the most troubled lives that was ever lived. Tempest and tumult, tumult and tempest, the waves breaking over it all the time, till the worn body was laid in the grave. But the inner life was a sea of glass. The great calm was always there. At any moment you might have gone to Him and found Rest.

September 4.

If a man does not exercise his arm he develops no biceps muscle ; and if a man does not exercise his soul, he requires no muscle in his soul, no strength of character, no vigor of moral fibre, nor beauty of spiritual guards.

September 5.

For a want of patience, a want of kindness, a want of generosity, a want of courtesy, a want of unselfishness, are all instantaneously symbolized in one flash of Temper.

September 6.

Christ never said much in mere words about the Christian Graces. He lived them, He was them. We learn His art by living with Him, like the old apprentices with their masters.

September 7.

Remain side by side with Him who loved us, and gave Himself for us, and you too will become a permanent magnet, a permanently attractive force; and like Him you will draw all men unto you, like Him you will be drawn unto all men. That is the inevitable effect of Love. Any man who fulfills that cause must have that effect produced in him.

September 8.

"Love does not behave itself unseemly." Politeness has been defined as love in trifles. Courtesy is said to be love in little things. And the one secret of politeness is to love.

September 9.

The test of religion, the final test of religion, is not religiousness, but Love. I say the final test of religion at that great Day is not religiousness, but Love; not what I have done, not what I have believed, not what I have achieved, but how I have discharged the common charities of life. Sins of commission in that awful indictment are not even referred to. By what we have not done, *by sins of omission*, we are judged. It could not be otherwise. For the withholding of love is the negation of the spirit of Christ, the proof that we never knew Him, that for us He lived in vain.

September 10.

Thank God the Christianity of to day is coming nearer the world's need. Live to help that on.

September 11.

The Gospel offers a man life. Never offer men a thimbleful of Gospel. Do not offer them merely joy, or merely peace, or merely rest, or merely safety; tell them how Christ came to give men a more abundant life than they have, a life abundant in love, and therefore abundant in salvation for themselves, and large in enterprise for the alleviation and redemption of the world. Then only can the Gospel take hold of the whole of a man, body, soul, and spirit, and give to each part of his nature its exercise and reward.

September 12.

What we are stretches past what we do, beyond what we possess.

September 13.

I do not think we ourselves are aware how much our religious life is made up of phrases; how much of what we call Christian experience is only a dialect of the Churches, a mere religious phraseology with almost nothing behind it in what we really feel and know.

September 14.

Put a seal upon your lips and forget what you have done. After you have been kind, after Love has stolen forth into the world and done its beautiful work, go back into the shade again and say nothing about it. Love hides even from itself.

September 15.

The ceaseless chagrin of a self-centred life can be removed at once by learning Meekness and Lowliness of heart. He who learns them is for ever proof against it. He lives henceforth a charmed life.

September 16.

Because He loved us, we love, we love everybody. Our heart is slowly changed. Contemplate the love of Christ, and you will love. Stand before that mirror, reflect Christ's character, and you will be changed into the same image from tenderness to tenderness. There is no other way.

September 17.

That is the supreme work to which we need to address ourselves in this world, to learn Love. Is life not full of opportunities for learning Love?

Every man and woman every day has a thousand of them.   The world is not a playground ; it is a schoolroom.   Life is not a holiday, but an education.   And the one eternal lesson for us all is *how better we can love.*

September 18.

You will give yourselves to many things, give yourself first to Love.   *Hold things in their proportion.*   Let at least the first great object of our lives be to achieve the character defended in these words, the character—and it is the character of Christ—which is built round Love.

September 19.

How can modern men to-day make Christ, the absent Christ, their most constant companion still ?   The answer is that Friendship is a spiritual thing.   It is independent of Matter, or Space, or Time.   That which I love in my friend is not that which I see. What influences me in my friend is not his body, but his spirit.

September 20.

The influences we meet are not simply held for a moment on the polished surface and thrown off again into space. Each is retained where first it fell, and stored up in the soul for ever.

September 21.

My hidden ideals of what is beautiful I have drawn from Christ.

September 22.

A Science without mystery is unknown ; a Religion without mystery is absurd. There is no attempt to reduce Religion to a question of mathematics, or demonstrate God in biological formulæ. The elimination of mystery from the universe is the elimination of Religion. However far the scientific method may penetrate the

Spiritual World, there will always remain a region to be explored by a scientific faith. "I shall never rise to the point of view which wishes to 'raise' faith to knowledge. To me the way of truth is to come through the knowledge of my ignorance to the submissiveness of faith, and then, making that my starting place, to raise my knowledge into faith."

September 23.

Character is a thing built up by slow degrees, that it is hourly changing for better or for worse, according to the images which flit across it.

September 24.

He that would be happy, let him remember that there is but one way—it is more blessed, it is more happy, to give than to receive.

September 25.

Theology is searching on every hand for an-

other echo of the Voice of which Revelation also
is the echo, that out of the mouths of two wit-
nesses its truths should be established.   That
other echo can only come from Nature.

September 26.

We have Truth in Nature as it came from God.
And it has to be read with the same unbiassed
mind, the same open eye, the same faith, and the
same reverence as all other Revelation.

September 27.

The soul, which has no correspondence with
the spiritual environment, is spiritually dead.   It
may be that it never possessed the spiritual eye or
the spiritual ear, or a heart which throbbed in
response to the love of God.   If so, having
never lived, it cannot be said to have died.   But
not to have these correspondences is to be in the
state of Death.   To the spiritual world, to the
Divine Environment, it is dead —as a stone which

has never lived is dead to the environment of the organic world.

September 28.

To every man who truly studies Nature there is a God.   Call Him by whatever name—a Creator, a Supreme Being, a Great First Cause, a Power that makes for Righteousness—Science has a God; and he who believes in this, in spite of all protest, possesses a theology.

September 29.

There is, for example, a Sense of Sight in the religious nature.   Neglect this, leave it undeveloped, and you never miss it.   You simply see nothing.   But develop it and you see God.   And the line along which to develop it is known to us. Become pure in heart.   The pure in heart shall see God.   Here, then, is one opening for soul-culture—the avenue through purity of heart to the spiritual seeing of God.

September 30.

Then there is a Sense of Sound. Neglect this, leave it undeveloped, and you never miss it. You simply hear nothing. Develop it, and you hear God. And the line along which to develop it is known to us. Obey Christ. Become one of Christ's flock. "The sheep hear His voice, and He calleth them by name." Here, then, is another opportunity for the culture of the soul—a gateway through the Shepherd's fold to hear the Shepherd's voice.

October 1.

And there is a Sense of Touch to be acquired—such a sense as the woman had who touched the hem of Christ's garment, that wonderful electric touch called faith, which moves the very heart of God.

October 2.

And there is a Sense of Taste—a spiritual hunger after God; a something within which

tastes and sees that He is good.   And there is
the talent for Inspiration.   Neglect that, and all
the scenery of the spiritual world is flat and
frozen.   And last of all there is the great capacity
for Love, even for the love of God—the expand-
ing capacity for feeling more and more its height
and depth, its length and breadth.   Till that is
felt no man can really understand that word, "so
great salvation," for what is its measure but that
other "so" of Christ—God so loved the world
that He gave His only begotten Son ?   Verily,
how shall we escape if we neglect that ?

October 3.

A doctor has no prescription for growth.   He
can tell me how growth may be stunted or impaired, but the process itself is recognized as beyond control—one of the few, and therefore very
significant, things which Nature keeps in her own
hands.   No physician of souls, in like manner,
has any prescription for spiritual growth.   It is

the question he is most often asked and most often answers wrongly. He may prescribe more earnestness, more prayer, more self-denial or more Christian work. These are prescriptions for something, but not for growth. Not that they may not encourage growth; but the soul grows as the lily grows, without trying, without fretting, without ever thinking. There *can* indeed be no other principle of growth than this. It is a vital act. And to try to *make* a thing grow is as absurd as to help the tide to come in or the sun rise.

October 4.

There are certain burrowing animals—the mole, for instance—which have taken to spending their lives beneath the surface of the ground. And Nature has taken her revenge upon them in a thoroughly natural way—she has closed up their eyes. If they mean to live in darkness, she argues, eyes are obviously a superfluous function. By neglecting them these animals made it clear

they do not want them. And as one of Nature's
fixed principles is that nothing shall exist in vain,
the eyes are presently taken away, or reduced to
.a rudimentary state. There are fishes also which
have had to pay the same terrible forfeit for having made their abode in dark caverns where eyes
can never be required. And in exactly the same
way the spiritual eye must die and lose its power
by purely natural law, if the soul chooses to walk
in darkness rather than in light.

October 5.

We have admitted that he who knows not God
may not be a monster; we cannot say he will not
be a dwarf. This precisely, and on perfectly
natural principles, is what he must be. You can
dwarf a soul just as you can dwarf a plant, by
depriving it of a full environment Such a soul
for a time may have "a name to live." Its character may betray no sign of atrophy. But its
very virtue somehow has the pallor of a flower

that is grown in darkness, or as the herb which has never seen the sun, no fragrance breathes from its spirit. To morality, possibly, this organism offers the example of an irreproachable life; but to science it is an instance of arrested development; and to religion it presents the spectacle of a corpse—a living Death. With Ruskin, "I do not wonder at what men suffer, but I wonder often at what they lose."

October 6.

The soul, in its highest sense, is a vast capacity for God. It is like a curious chamber added on to being, and somehow involving being, a chamber with elastic and contractile walls, which can be expanded, with God as its guest, illimitably, but which without God shrinks and shrivels until every vestige of the Divine is gone, and God's image is left without God's Spirit. One cannot call what is left a soul; it is a shrunken, useless organ, a capacity sentenced to death by disuse.

Nature has her revenge upon neglect as well as upon extravagance. Misuse, with her, is as mortal a sin as abuse.

October 7.

I say that man believes in a God, who feels himself in the presence of a Power which is not himself, and is immeasurably above himself, a Power in the contemplation of which he is absorbed, in the knowledge of which he finds safety and happiness.

October 8.

Sin is simply apostasy from God, unbelief in God. "Sin is manifest in its true character when the demand of holiness in the conscience, presenting itself to the man as one of loving submission to God, is put from him with aversion. Here sin appears as it really is, a turning away from God; and while the man's guilt is enhanced, there ensues a benumbing of the heart resulting from the crushing of those higher impulses. This is what is meant by the reprobate state of those who reject Christ and will not believe the Gospel, so often spoken of in the New Testament; this unbelief is just the closing of the heart against the highest love."

October 9.

If sin is estrangement from God, this very estrangement is Death. It is a want of correspondence. If sin is selfishness, it is conducted at the expense of life. Its wages are Death—"he that loveth his life," said Christ, "shall lose it."

October 10.

This law, which is true for the whole plant-world, is also valid for the animal and for man. Air is not life, but corruption—so literally corruption that the only way to keep out corruption, when life has ebbed, is to keep out air. Life is merely a temporary suspension of these destructive powers; and this is truly one of the most accurate definitions of life we have yet received—

"the sum total of the functions which resist death."

Spiritual life, in like manner, is the sum total of the functions which resist sin   The soul's atmosphere is the daily trial, circumstance, and temptation of the world.   And as it is life alone which gives the plant power to utilize the elements, and as, without it, they utilize it, so it is the spiritual life alone which gives the soul power to utilize temptation and trial ; and without it they destroy the soul.   How shall be escape if we refuse to exercise these functions—in other words, if we neglect?

October 11.

To correspond with the God of Science, the Eternal Unknowable, would be everlasting existence ; to correspond with "the true God and Jesus Christ," is Eternal Life.   The quality of the Eternal Life alone makes the heaven ; mere everlastingness might be no boon.   Even the brief span of the temporal life is too long for those who

spend its years in sorrow.   Time itself, let alone
Eternity, is all but excruciating to Doubt.   And
many besides Schopenhauer have secretly regarded
consciousness as the hideous mistake and malady
of Nature.   Therefore we must not only have
quantity of years, to speak in the language of the
present, but quality of correspondence.   When
we leave Science behind, this correspondence also
receives a higher name.   It becomes communion.
Other names there are for it, religious and theo-
logical.   It may be included in a general expression, Faith; or we may call it by a personal and
specific term, Love.

October 12.

The punishment of sin is inseparably bound
up with itself.   To refuse to deny one's self is just
to be left with the self undenied.   The discipline
of life was meant to destroy this self, but that discipline having been evaded, its purpose is balked.
But the soul is the loser.   In seeking to gain its

life it has really lost it. This is what Christ meant when He said : " He that loveth his life shall lose it, and he that hateth his life in this world shall keep it unto life eternal."

October 13.

No truth of Christianity has been more ignorantly or wilfully travestied than the doctrine of Immortality. The popular idea, in spite of a hundred protests, is that Eternal Life is to live forever. A single glance at the *locus classicus*, might have made this error impossible. There we are told that Life Eternal is not to live. This is Life Eternal—*to know*.

October 14.

The well-defined spiritual life is not only the highest life, but its is also the most easily lived. The whole cross is more easily carried than the half. It is the man who tries to make the best of both worlds who makes nothing of either.

13

And he who seeks to serve two masters misses the benediction of both.   But he who has taken his stand, who has drawn a boundary line, sharp and deep about his religious life, who has marked off all beyond as forever forbidden ground to him, finds the yoke easy and the burden light.

October 15.

My thoughts of what is manly, and noble, and pure, have almost all of them arisen from the Lord Jesus Christ.

October 16.

The creation of a new heart, the renewing of a right spirit, is an omnipotent work of God. Leave it to the Creator. " He which hath began a good work in you will perfect it unto that day."

October 17.

The one thing which Christianity tries to extirpate from a man's nature is selfishness, even though it be the losing of his own soul.

October 18.

We can only see a very little bit at a time; and we must, I think, learn to believe that other men can see bits of truth as well as ourselves.

October 19.

It is only one of the aims of Christianity to make the best men.   The next thing Christ wants to do is to make the best world.   And He tries to make the best world by setting the best men loose upon the world to influence it and reflect Him upon it.

October 20.

Friendship is the nearest thing we know to what religion is.   God is love.   And to make religion akin to Friendship is simply to give it the highest expression conceivable by man.

October 21.

Thorough Bible study is of such importance. We can get to the bottom of truth in itself, and be able to give a reason for the faith that is in us.

October 22.

All my conceptions of the progress of grace in the soul; all the steps by which the divine life is evolved; all the ideals that overhang the blessed sphere which awaits us beyond this world—these are derived from the Saviour. The life that I now live in the flesh I live by the faith of the Son of God.

October 23.

Live in peace and harmony and brotherliness with every one.

October 24.

Christ is the Light of the world, and much of His Light is reflected from things in the world.

October 25.

It is when drawing near the Lord Jesus
Christ, and longing to be loved, that I have
the most vivid sense of unsymmetry, of imper-
fection, of absolute unworthiness, and of my
sinfulness.   Character and conduct are never so
vividly set before me as when in silence I bend
in the presence of Christ. revealed not in wrath,
but in the love to me.   I never so much long to
be lovely, that I may be loved, as when I have
this revelation or Christ before my mind.

October 26.

Christ shines through men, through books.
through history, through nature, music, art.
Look for Him there.

October 27.

Heredity and Environment are the master-
influences of the organic world.   These have

made all of us what we are.   These forces are still
ceaselessly playing upon all our lives.   And he
who truly understands these influences; he who
has decided how much to allow to each ; he who
can regulate new forces as they arise, or adjust
them to the old, so directing them as at one
moment to make them co-operate, at another to
counteract one another, understands the rationale
of personal development.   To seize continuously
the opportunity of more and more perfect adjust-
ment to better and higher conditions, to balance
some inward evil with some purer influence acting
from without, in a word to make our Environment at the same time that it is making us—these
are the secrets of a well-ordered and successful
life.

October 28,

I have had a hunger to be loved of Christ.   You
all know, in some relations, what it is to be hungry for love.   Your heart seems unsatisfied until
you can draw something more toward you from

those that are dearest to you.   There have been times when I have had an unspeakable heart-hunger for Christ's love.

October 29.

The cardinal error in the religious life is to attempt to live without an environment.   Spirit-ual experience occupies itself, not too much, but too exclusively, with one factor—the soul.   We delight in dissecting this much tortured faculty, from time to time, in search of a certain some-thing which we call our faith—forgetting that faith is but an attitude, an empty Hand for grasp-ing an environing Presence.

October 30.

Why do we seek to breathe without an atmos-phere, to drink without a well?   Why this unsci-entific attempt to sustain life for weeks at a time without an Environment?   It is because we have never truly seen the necessity for an Environment.

We have not been working with a principle. We are told to "wait only upon God," but we do not know why. It has never been as clear to us that without God the soul will die as that without food the body will perish.

October 31.

"As the branch cannot bear fruit of itself except it abide in the vine, no more can ye, except ye abide in Me." The word here, it will be observed again, is *cannot*. It is the imperative of natural law. Fruit-bearing without Christ is not an improbability, but an impossibility. As well expect the natural fruit to flourish without air and heat, without soil and sunshine.

November 1.

Whatever energy the soul expands must first be "taken into it from without." We are not Creators, but creatures; God is our refuge *and strength*. Communion with God, therefore, is a scientific necessity; and nothing will more help the defeated spirit which is struggling in the wreck of its religious life than a common-sense hold of this plain biological principle that without Environment he can do nothing.

November 2.

Nature is not more natural to my body than God is to my soul. Every animal and plant has its own Environment. And the further one inquires into the relations of the one to the other, the more one sees the marvellous intricacy and beauty of the adjustments.

November 3.

The psalmist's "God is our refuge and strength" is only the earlier form, less defined, less practicable, but not less noble, of Christ's "Come unto Me, and I will give you rest."

November 4.

The Life of the Senses, high and low, may perfect itself in Nature. Even the Life of thought may find a large complement in surrounding things. But the higher thought, and the conscience, and the religious Life, can only perfect themselves in God.

November 5.

The New Testament is nowhere more impressive than where it insists on the fact of man's independence. In its view the first step in religion is for man to feel his helplessness. Christ's first beatitude is to the poor in spirit.

November 6.

It is easier to criticise the best thing superbly than to do the smallest thing indifferently.

November 7.

"An idle life," says Goethe, "is death anticipated." Better far be burned at the stake of Public Opinion than die the living death of Parasitism. Better an aberrant theology than a suppressed organization. Better a little faith dearly won, better launched alone on the infinite bewilderment of Truth, than perish on the splendid plenty of the richest creeds.

November 8.

Who is to help these people? No one can lift them up in any way except those who are living the life of Christ, and it is their privilege and business to bind up the broken-hearted.

November 9.

The most obvious lesson in Christ's teaching is that there is no happiness in having and getting anything, but only in giving.

November 10.

It is not a strange thing, then, for the soul to

find its life in God.   This is its native air.   God
as the Environment of the soul has been from the
remotest age the doctrine of all the deepest
thinkers in religion.   And long before it was
possible for religion to give scientific expression
to its greatest truths, men of insight uttered
themselves in psalms which could not have been
truer to Nature had the most modern light con-
trolled the inspiration.   "As the hart panteth
after the water-brooks, so panteth my soul after
Thee, O God."

November 11.

Our companionship with Him, like all true
companionship, is a spiritual communion.   All
friendship, all love, human and Divine, is purely
spiritual.

November 12.

There is no more important lesson that we
have to carry with us than that truth is not to be

found in what I have been taught. That is not truth. Truth is not what I have been taught.

November 13.

Theology is the most abstruse thing in the world, but practical religion is the simplest thing.

November 14.

You will find as you look back upon your life that the moments that stand out, the moments when you have really lived, are the moments when you have done things in a spirit of love.

November 15.

Religion is not a strange or added thing, but the inspiration of the secular life, the breathing of an eternal spirit through this temporal world.

November 16.

If the Christian is to " live unto God," he

must "die unto sin." If he does not kill sin, sin will inevitably kill him.

November 17.

The entire dependence of the soul upon God is not an exceptional mystery, nor is man's helplessness an arbitrary and unprecedented phenomenon. It is the law of all Nature.

November 18.

To become like Christ is the only thing in the world worth caring for, the thing before which every ambition of man is folly, and all lower achievement vain.

November 19.

The highest and manliest character that ever lived was Christ.

November 20.

Religion must ripen its fruit for every temperament : and the way even unto its highest heights must be by a gateway through which the peoples of the world may pass.

November 21.

It is the beautiful work of Christianity everywhere to adjust the burden of life to those who bear it, and them to it.

November 22.

For a few short hours you live the Eternal Life. The eternal life, the life of faith, is simply the life of the higher vision.

November 23.

Patience ; kindness ; generosity ; humility ; courtesy ; unselfishness ; good temper ; guilelessness ; sincerity—these make up the supreme gift, the stature of the perfect man.

November 24.

Every hour a *kingdom* is coming in your heart,

in your home, in the world near you, be it a kingdom of darkness or a kingdom of light.

November 25.

It is the Law of Influence that *we become like those whom we habitually admire.*

November 26.

A man's Christianity does not consist in merely his own soul, but in sanctifying and purifying the lives of his fellow-men.

November 27.

Stupendous victory and mystery of regeneration that mortal man should suggest to the world, *God!*

November 28.

The Spiritual Life is the gift of the Living Spirit. The spiritual man is no mere development of the natural man. He is a new creation born from above.

November 29.

Faith is an attitude—a mirror set at the right angle.

November 30.

The Christian life is the only life that will ever be completed. Apart from Christ the life of man is a broken pillar, the race of men an unfinished pyramid. One by one, in sight of Eternity, all human Ideals fall short; one by one, before the open grave all human hopes dissolve. The Laureate sees a moment's light in Nature's jealousy for the Type; but that too vanishes.

> " 'So careful of the type?' but no
> From scarped cliff and quarried stone
> She cries, ' A thousand types are gone;
> I care for nothing, all shall go."

All shall go? No, one Type remains. "Whom He did foreknow He did also predestinate to be conformed to the Image of His Son." And " when Christ, who is our life, shall appear, then shall ye also appear with Him in glory."

14

December 1.

No form of vice, not worldliness, not greed of gold, not drunkenness itself, does more to un-Christianize society than evil temper.

December 2.

To be trusted is to be saved. And if we try to influence or elevate others, we shall soon see that success is in proportion to their belief of our belief in them.

December 3.

My sense of sin is never strong when I think of the law; my sense of sin is strong when I think of love.

December 4.

No fever can attack a perfectly sound body; no fever of unrest can disturb a soul which has breathed the air or learned the ways of Christ.

December 5.

You can take nothing greater to the world than

the impress and reflection of the Love of God
upon your own character

December 6.

Sanctity is in character, and not in moods;
Divinity in our own plain calm humanity, and in
no mystic rapture of the soul.

December 7.

Christian men are the salt of the earth in the
most literal sense. They, and they alone, keep
the world from utter destruction.

December 8.

Paul tells us that if we live in Christ we are
changed into His image. All that a man has to
do, then, to be like Christ, is simply to live in
friendship with Christ, and the character follows.

December 9.

Character is to wear forever; who will wonder
or grudge that it cannot be developed in a day?

December 10.

We can make no progress without the full use of all the intellectual powers that God has endowed us with.

December 11.

For more than twenty-five years I instinctively have gone to Christ to draw a measure and a rule for everything.

December 12.

The Bible is a product of religion, not a cause of it.

December 13.

Every character has an inward spring, let Christ be it. Every action has a key-note, let Christ set it.

December 14.

Whatever rest is provided by Christianity for the children of God, it is certainly never contemplated that it should supersede personal effort. And any rest which ministers to indifference is immoral and unreal—it makes parasites and not men. Just because God worketh in him, as the evidence and triumph of it, the true child of God works out his own salvation—works it out having really received it—not as a light thing, a superfluous labor, but with fear and trembling as a reasonable and indispensable service.

December 15.

Faith is never opposed to reason in the New Testament, but to sight.

December 16.

Nothing that happens in the world happens by chance.

December 17.

Above all, let us remember to hold the truth in love. That is the most sanctifying influence of all.

December 18.

In will-power, in mere spasms of earnestness there is no salvation.

December 19.

Reflect the character of Christ, and you will become like Christ.

December 20.

Death to the lower self, is the nearest gate and the quickest road to life.

December 21.

Whatever else Christ claimed to be or to do, He at least knew how to live.

December 22.

Suppose now it be granted for a moment that the character of the not-a-Christian is as beautiful as that of the Christian. This is simply to say that the crystal is as beautiful as the organism. One is quite entitled to hold this ; but what he is not entitled to hold is that both in the same sense are living. *He that hath the Son hath Life, and he that hath not the Son of God hath not Life.*

And in the face of this law, no other conclusion is possible than that that which is flesh remains flesh. No matter how great the development of beauty, that which is flesh is withal flesh. The elaborateness or the perfection of the moral development in any given instance can do nothing to break down this distinction.

December 23.

Mark well the splendor of this idea of salvation. It is not merely final "safety," to be forgiven sin, to evade the curse. It is not, vaguely, "to get to heaven." It is to be conformed to the Image of the Son. It is for these poor elements to attain to the Supreme Beauty. The organizing Life being Eternal, so must this Beauty be immortal. Its progress towards the Immaculate is already guaranteed. And more than all there is here fulfilled the sublimest of all prophecies; not Beauty alone but Unity is secured by the Type— Unity of man and man, God and man, God and Christ and man, till "all shall be one."

December 24.

Yet this is what Christianity is for—to teach men the Art of Life.   And its whole curriculum lies in one word—" Learn of Me."

December 25.

Live after Christ, in His Spirit, as in His Presence, and it is difficult to think what more you can do.

December 26.

After all, the best test for Life is just *living*. And living consists, as we have formerly seen, in corresponding with Environment.   Those therefore who find within themselves, and regularly exercise, the faculties for corresponding with the Divine Environment, may be said to live the Spiritual Life.

December 27.

The inward nature must develop out according to its Type, until the consummation of oneness with God is reached.

December 28.

O preposterous and vain man, thou who couldest not make a finger nail of thy body, thinkest thou to fashion this wonderful, mysterious, subtle soul of thine after the ineffable Image? Wilt thou ever permit thyself *to be* conformed to the Image of the Son? Wilt thou, who canst not add a cubit to thy stature, submit *to be* raised by the Type-Life within thee to the perfect stature of Christ?

December 29.

If to live with men, diluted to the millionth degree with the virtue of the Highest, can exalt and purify the nature, what bounds can be set to the influence of Christ?

December 30.

The recognition of the Ideal is the first step in the direction of Conformity. But let it be clearly observed that it is but a step. There is no vital connection between merely seeing the Ideal and

being conformed to it.   Thousands admire Christ
who never become Christians.

December 31.

The work begun by Nature is finished by the
Supernatural—as we are wont to call the higher
natural.   And as the veil is lifted by Christianity
it strikes men dumb with wonder.   For the goal
of Evolution is Jesus Christ.

www.ingramcontent.com/pod-product-compliance
Lightning Source LLC
Chambersburg PA
CBHW030132030726
47498CB00007B/2662